I0771740

Liabetes

Shanna M. Heath

Copyright © 2025 by Shanna M. Heath

All rights reserved.

No part of this book may be reproduced in any form or by any electronic or mechanical means, including information storage and retrieval systems, without written permission from the author, except for the use of brief quotations in a book review.

Contents

To our Redeemer, who is SO MUCH bigger than any mistake we could ever make.

And, of course, to my loving family.

Prologue

Poor as a Church Mouse

Nine. That's how old I was when I realized my family didn't have as much as most. This occurred to me in third grade, when my best friend Xavier and I went to Lexington Comic-Con with his uncle and dad. They couldn't wait for us to meet their favorite actors from *Star Gladiators*. We're talking giddy males in full-on nerd-out costumes and everything. I was too young to care that I was accompanying men dressed in spandex and pleather while we ate mutant turkey legs from food trucks on Short Street. And of course we had ice cream. Xavier has always lived for ice cream.

I used the last of my change I'd saved from weeks of chores to buy a giant waffle cone filled with double scoops—we ordered different flavors and then shared, because best friends don't have cooties and we got to try more flavors that way.

We met the star of the series, Will Richards, in real life. He even signed Pastor Reyes' special edition DVD cover, still wrapped in yellowed cellophane, that he'd bought over two decades ago at some place called Blockbuster and kept in pristine condition "for such a time as this." His words...

But I was truly enlightened about my destitute state after Xavier and I stumbled upon the *Guardians of the Faith* comic book table. I'd never seen such stunning graphics in all my nine years, and I loved to draw and color. The powerful emotions evident on the characters' faces, the vivid colors, the movement and energy. Wowza. And in shiny font on the cover was the illustrator's name: Paige O'Donnell. She became my official Shero. I became convinced I was destined to follow in her footsteps.

Various *Guardians of the Faith* paraphernalia were displayed on the table, including art kits, bobblehead dolls of each Guardian, and—my favorite—massive, framed panels signed by the comic illustrators, O'Donnell included. When Xavier's dad and Uncle Angelo caught up with us, Xavier asked if he could have a copy of a comic, while I salivated at the thought of taking home the fancy-colored pencils and *How to Draw the Guardians of the Faith* book.

Pastor Reyes squeaked his wallet out from his entirely too-tight man leggings and slid a crisp twenty-dollar bill across the table, and just like that, my bestie became the proud owner of the special edition, mylar-protected issue thirty-one. I offered my buddy a toothy grin, happy he'd gotten his comic and certain we'd *ooh* and *ahh* in admiration all the way home.

Since I'd used the last of my money on the steroid-laced drumstick and irrationally large ice cream cone, I wondered if I could find a book like the one on the table at the library for free.

"Awa," Xavier said, a solemn look in his deep brown eyes as he spoke to his dad.

Pastor Reyes' expression softened in response. "Awa."

Then he surprised me by sliding another couple of bills to the glossy-eyed employee working the register. I couldn't believe it when she bagged up the pencils and book and gave it to me. *Me.* Xavier's Uncle Angelo chuckled and mussed my hair.

It was dark by the time we loaded up Pastor Reyes' hatchback to leave Comic-Con, and Xavier drifted off before we got out of the parking lot. I rested my head on the back of my seat and closed my eyes, but I couldn't sleep. I was far too excited about the contents of the bag clutched in my arms, and a little nervous that I'd get in trouble with Mom and Dad for accepting such a lavish gift. Pastor Reyes and Angelo must have thought I'd crashed like Xavier, because they were soon talking in hushed tones.

"Awa? Treating a kid to overpriced pencils and a book isn't exactly compassion," Angelo whispered quietly.

"Awa as in charity, Angelo. Olivia's a sweet, brilliant girl–" Then the pastor sighed heavily and continued, "–and she's as poor as a church mouse."

I froze, afraid to move.

"Is she really? Huh, I had no idea."

"The Jameses are good, hard-working people, they just struggle. One step forward, two steps back. They remind me of our magpinsan before we left Balanga."

Based on Angelo's low, drawn-out whistle that followed, I'd guessed that meant we were, in fact, pretty poor.

I knew I sometimes did without, especially being the youngest of three, but I didn't know I was *poor* poor until that moment. One meager level up from destitute, based on Angelo's reaction.

I'm Olivia James, smart as a tack and poor as a church mouse. But this mouse has dreams and my hopes for the future are brighter than the Prisma brand colored pencils I squeezed tight that night.

Chapter 1
The Frequency Illusion

"Stop eating all the hard candies, Olivia. Other students might want one, too." Mrs. Carlson, my guidance counselor, shoos my hand away from her ceramic candy dish, then continues to comb through my college information on her MacBook. "I usually have to encourage students to narrow down their choices at this point in the year, but you seem pretty set on Vanderbilt."

"Is that a bad thing?" I twist the ends of a watermelon Jolly Rancher wrapper. "Vandy's always been my dream school."

"Dream school or not, it's never a bad idea to have a back-up plan."

"You don't think I'll get in?" I bite my bottom lip and try not to allow my apprehension to overwhelm me. My grades are stellar and I'm involved in more extracurricular activities than both my brothers ever were—combined—but waiting to hear back from admissions is worse than waiting for Christmas.

She pauses her typing and looks at me from across her cluttered desk. "Oh honey, I have no doubt you'll get in. It's the financial aid I'm worried about." She shakes her head and her forehead wrinkles crease behind her stylish readers.

That makes two of us. A familiar panic in my stomach starts tying knots with my small intestine. I'm painfully aware that I have a dream school and a nightmare budget.

"Vandy being out-of-state doesn't help. You've already started the FAFSA process with your parents?"

"Yes ma'am." Ugh. Vandy is less than an hour from the Kentucky state line.

"And you registered with Fastweb like I recommended?"

"Yep." The only thing I've won from that website so far is a motherload of junk mail, but Mrs. Carlson has been rooting for me, so I keep that to myself. Wouldn't want to hurt her feelings.

"Alright, Miss James," she sighs as the printer roars to life. "I'll continue to help search for scholarships and you keep your grades up. Sign here and I'll be right back." She taps her polished pointer finger next to the student signature line on the Seniors January Check-In form then walks out to the office's main suite.

I scribble my name across the bottom and sit back in the chair. Snippets of her conversation drift through the door and I can tell it might be a while. Something about two sophomores disrupting biology for a weird TikTok trend.

My mind wanders as I worry about financial aid and my eyes roam around her quirky office. She has pictures of her family, mental health journals, fidget toys, pictures of past graduates, and a cartoon I drew of her beside her desk to thank her for helping me through the great prom fiasco of Junior year. I'd illustrated her as Wonder Woman, saving my day.

Finally, my gaze lands on a packet peeking out from the bottom of a stack of papers on the edge of her desk.

Wonderbrink Foundation Diabetes Scholarship: $15,000

I pull my unruly auburn waves into a messy bun, slide the stapled packet my way, and continue reading.

Eligibility applies to any high school senior with Type 1 diabetes who actively participates on an organized sports or athletic team. The Wonderbrink Foundation will award three scholarships up to $15,000 each, renewed annually for up to four years, to students who successfully manage their diabetes with medication, exercise, and a healthy diet. Students must submit an online application, a letter of recommendation from a current teacher, and a 500-word essay requirement. More information is available on the Wonderbrink Foundation website. Application deadline: March 1.

Interesting. This is the first time I've ever considered myself at a disadvantage for not having a disability. Why does college have to be so expensive? And how are my brothers paying for it?

With scholarships, that's what. Clark's brilliant, and

Matt's no dummy, but sports are paying his bills. He caught the eye of the college football scouts as early as his freshman year. I glance back at the papers. I'm good at soccer, but not great, and I'm certainly smart, but my real talents include art, art, and more art. Well, not all art. My attempts at the pottery wheel led to a set of Hobbit dishes, so I've stuck to illustrations.

The door flies open, startling me, and I shove the thin packet into my backpack. Why did I do that? It's not like I can pull it out and put it back on her desk.

"I'd love to stay and chat a little longer, but you've got to get back to fourth period." She scribbles out a hall pass, rips the small paper from its pad, and hands it to me. "We shouldn't keep Mr. Winters waiting. I've got to run to Barkley Pediatrics and check on a student. Seems a social media challenge went south pretty fast."

Yikes.

The keys on her lanyard jingle as she ushers me out and heads off.

* * *

Fourth-period psychology is, by far, my favorite class. It's veritable brain candy and it gives me a break from the rigors of my core classes. And our teacher's southern accent is strong—thick like honey. If "kindness" had a sound, his voice would be it.

I sneak in and take my seat after the tardy bell rings. Mr. Winters clears his throat. "Y'all get on Google Classroom and scroll down to our Unit on Cognitive Processes. Today we're going to discuss the Baader-Meinhof

Phenomenon, otherwise known as the Frequency Illu-sion." He combs his hand down his neatly trimmed salt-n-pepper beard and paces the front of the room.

"Y'all ever hear of something new–never heard of it in your life–and then all of a sudden you keep hearing it over and over again? Might pop up in conversation or you hear it on one of them reels you kids are always watching. That's what I'm talking about. If y'all intentionally change what you think about, what you start to notice will change too."

Some of my classmates start to mumble, skeptical of Mr. Winters' claim.

"I thought that only happened when I whispered something near my phone." My buddy Xavier's not wrong. He gives me a wink and I roll my eyes. We've been over this. Best friends don't wink at each other. I'd like to pretend that, unlike all the other girls at this school, I'm immune to his charms. That couldn't be farther from the truth, but I'm taking that little scrap of information to my grave.

"No, son. You're thinking about algorithms, but I'm talking about psychology. Y'all ever notice a nice new car? Never seen one like it before. Then you see it every-where—ad on your Chromebook, somebody's shirt, heck, your neighbor's driveway. That's the Frequency Illusion. It's a cognitive bias that affects how y'all think and process information." Mr. Winters picks up a stack of papers from his desk and starts to distribute them.

"Y'all are going to work with your table groups to complete a scavenger hunt of sorts. I've written an obscure term or phrase at the top of your paper. You will have fifteen minutes to walk around the school to find instances of y'all's assigned chosen object or concept. Don't forget a hall pass."

As our classmates start to shuffle towards the door, I steal a glance at the paper my shoulder partner Jimmy has picked up. My group's been given the term "Interface." Xavier, Amber, Jimmy—my fearless table comrades —and I, stroll the halls. Amber walks beside me as she looks up a definition on her phone. I peek down at the Merriam-Webster page she has pulled up on her screen, aware I'm a Neanderthal compared to her short five feet.

We meander past Mrs. Johnson's English Lit class and overhear a ninth-grader's presentation. "In George Orwell's *Animal Farm*, the pigs like, totally manipulated language and used propaganda as, like, an interface to control the other animals..." I stop in my tracks and look at Xavier. Goosebumps scatter across my arms. Did that really just happen?

Weird.

Down the next hallway, we pass Mr. Henderson's class, now rid of any trace of TikTok shenanigans, and they're watching a documentary. The commentator's nasally, monotone voice floats down the hall... "The cell membrane serves as the interface between the cell's internal environment and the external surroundings..." The Baader-Meinhof Phenomenon is legit. On our return trip to Mr. Winter's class, we overhear two freshmen on the E-sports team at their lockers talking about the interface on the new PlayStation.

But something else strange happens, too. I have my own experience with the Illusion Principle. It taunts me.

We pass the nurses' station and a poster for a diabetes information number calls out to me. Never noticed that before. I do a double take when we pass a window looking out to the student parking lot and I spy Nick Jonas' face as part of a "Slow down sugar, I'm diabetic," sticker on the bumper of a dinged-up Prius. I've seen the driver shoving Sour Patch Kids in her pie-hole as she parks on multiple occasions, so there's no way that's a personal reference. Maybe she's just an IconNick? But talk about a weird interface.

"You coming, Liv?" Xavier's question pulls me out of my stupor. I'm not even sure when I stopped walking.

"She's too busy checking out your Filipino tan. Is someone a little jelly?" Jimmy exaggerates a fake elbow to Xavier's ribs and waggles his brows. Amber rolls her eyes.

Jealous? No. Appreciative? Absolutely. Not that I'd share that little tidbit out loud. Xavier wears a grin that suggests maybe I *should* covet his perpetual summer glow, so I counter Jimmy with, "Oh puh-lease. Don't act like you don't love my pasty white porcelain skin, dotted with these glorious freckles."

I'd like to pretend my comeback quiets Jimmy right up, but I'm pretty sure he's just too bored with me to offer a witty retort. We head back to Mr. Winters' room where we take our seats and report our findings. Mr. Winters assigns a digital journal entry for homework, asking us to consider how understanding the Baader-Meinhof Phenomenon might impact our awareness in the future.

"...Two-hundred and fifty words, double spaced, Times New Roman font."

I try not to space out as he gives the specifics, but my mind drifts back to the diabetes situation.

With only about five minutes left before the dismissal bell is scheduled to ring, I open a new document to get an early start on the assignment. Xavier places a pale blue sticky note on the edge of my binder, a tiny number nineteen scribbled in the top corner, a large capital letter B in the center. From my peripheral vision, it appears Jimmy didn't get one, neither did Amber. A quick glance at Xavier and he seems to be biting his lip to keep from grinning.

I gesture to the note and raise my shoulders. He lifts both his hands as if to suggest "I don't know." Then he whispers, "You should decorate it."

Boys are weird, but bestie gets what bestie wants, so I attempt my finest doodle. Inspired by the January weather, snowflakes dot the post-it and the "B" becomes a lopsided, whimsical snowman. He has hearts for eyes and a sweet little grin on his round face. I'm considering what to make of the tiny number nineteen when the bell rings. I grab the note and start to hand it back to Xavier.

"Keep it. Actually, don't lose it." His long pinky finger pokes out as he threads his other arm through his backpack.

"Um, ok. Pinky promise." We shake digits, and he shakes his head. Then he helps load up my notebook and gives a loose red curl a tiny tug. It bounces back like a slinky.

"Later, Liv."

I stare as he walks off to fifth period. What was that all about?

* * *

Our mudroom separates the garage from the kitchen space, and I drop a laundry bag of dirty soccer pennies in front of the washing machine as I make my way inside. My brother's bags sit packed and waiting by the door.

"You guys are still here?" I thought I was coming home to an empty house after practice. Guess not. Most of my friends can't tell my twin older brothers apart, but I think they look completely different. Clark has a slight crook to his nose and Matt's hair is a tinge darker.

"Awww...We love you too, sis." Matt pulls out a chair so I can join them, but not until after he and Clark offer up an "Olivia Ovation." They flank each side, then envelop me in a giant bear hug. It's obnoxious and wonderful. They started this when I was a toddler and I don't even try to pretend like I'm annoyed by it.

I squeeze my way free of their embrace. "You guys know I love you. I thought you were both already on your way back to school." If college winter break is this long, that's just another reason to want to go.

"Uncle Lonnie still making you do laundry for your spot on the team?"

"Ahem. That's *Coach* Lonnie, and of course he is." Dad made a deal with his brother that I'd contribute to the team in tangible ways in lieu of a reduced monthly fee. Laundry, uniform prep, and nepotism gained me a spot on Pennyrile Lady Storm. He'd also have me run extra laps if I ever slipped up and called him "Uncle Lonnie" instead of "Coach."

"You still have that old Vanderbilt sweatshirt?" Clark

13

draws in a long, drawn-out whistle and I tug at the hem, suddenly insecure with my top of choice. They're both wearing hoodies from their respective colleges, swag that evokes envy. Matt in a Western Kentucky Football hoodie, and Clark in a Rhodes crew. I asked once if they could still feel their twin senses tingling from different states, and of course they said "No" at the same time. We share hand-me-down ginger genes, all sporting a similar shade of auburn wavy locks, more copper than carrot orange. Matt and Clark could be the Weasley twins—in both appearances and mischievousness.

Matt's eyes grow wide when he takes in my apparel. "I can't believe you still have that thing. If I didn't know better, I'd think Paige O'Donnell was wrapped in it at birth."

"No joke," Clark joins in. "You treat that thing like it's sacred."

"I absolutely do not." It is revered—threadbare and faded—but it isn't sacred. Ms. O'Donnell is the premier political cartoonist of our time, a Vanderbilt alum, and a huge inspiration to me. She's one of the main reasons I fell in love with illustrative arts in the first place, and I'm honing my skills to follow in her footsteps.

I playfully muss Matt's hair as I walk to the fridge and grab a Gatorade.

Matt swats my hand away. "I thought you had to work today?"

"Lucky for you two, I'm off. Where's mom and dad?" And dinner?

As if I had the power to somehow summon them, the garage door rumbles, followed shortly by the back door opening and shutting, bringing our parents into the kitchen. Pippa, our rescue mutt, is right behind them, her yellow tail wagging so hard it makes an adorable thumping sound against the cabinets.

"I must be living right if all three of my kiddos are home at the same time, already sitting around the table." Mom squishes us together—again—and my brothers feign exaggerated gagging sounds as they're subjected to another sweaty, post-soccer sister hug.

"You're just in time for our roast." Matt grabs a two-liter of soda from Dad and rubs Pippa's head.

"Roast? I had a coupon and we picked up pizza. We talked about this." Dad's face scrunches in confusion as he sets the boxes on the counter.

"Not that kind of roast. We're teasing Olivia for not burning the Vandy sweatshirt she got at Goodwill in sixth grade." He turns my way and offers an impish grin.

Mom stops filling glasses with ice to turn and reprimand my brothers. "Boys, leave your sister alone."

"But *mooooooommmm*, it's so much fun." As if Clark would ever miss an opportunity to goad me.

Matt taps his chin with his pointer finger and looks to the ceiling. "I bet Paige O'Donnell would have already been admitted to Vandy..."

I give him a look and bite my bottom lip, silently pleading with him not to go there. Thankfully, he nods, letting me know the message is received. My shoulders relax.

Clark, however, is not as astute as Matt and misses my glance of desperation. "Do you think Mom and Dad worry you might end up living in the basement at thirty? A boomerang baby?"

Like we even have a basement...

"Boys." Dad lifts his Irish-red eyebrows, his signature "I mean it" glare. He looks like an angry leprechaun no one in their right mind would mess with.

"She knows we're kidding, right Clark?" I do? Thank goodness for Matt's perceptiveness. Clark? Not so much.

"At least I didn't choose a college based on their female-to-male ratio." Clark is super intelligent, but he's also a bit of a ladies' man. But as much as I'd love to give him a hard time, he chose Rhodes mostly because he earned a Cambridge Scholarship. He's practically full ride.

Clark scoffs. "Ouch, Liv, that stings! Are you suggesting we didn't choose wisely? And since you're dead set on Vandy, aren't you waiting for *them* to choose *you*?"

Ugh. "You should have gone to clown college." It's a generic, pathetic response.

Clark doesn't miss a beat. "I'd be adorable juggling bowling pins in rainbow wigs."

"Sure you would. You can still pursue that dream if Plan A doesn't work out." I roll my eyes. *Brothers.* They're relentless.

Clark raises his slice of pizza. "To Plan B, then! And may our little Liv find a college that's better than clown school, Vandy or not."

Matt puts an arm around the back of my chair and leans in to offer some quiet encouragement. "We're teasing, Liv. You'll hear from Vandy soon."

"Thanks." Embarrassed that his small act of nurturing causes me to tear up, I divert my attention to Pippa and sneak her chunks of sausage from my pizza slices. Who could deny those big brown puppy eyes? The measured beating of her tail against the wall picks up, and I'm able to smile again.

Dad and Mom load the dishwasher after dinner while my brothers take the trash out and wipe the table clean. I'm feeding Pippa, who for *some reason* isn't hungry.

"Liv, I know you're worried about scholarships, but your mother and I will make it work." Wouldn't it be nice if I could fake that kind of confidence. I appreciate Dad's comfort, but now that dang lump is back in my throat.

"How did your meeting with the guidance counselor go today? Any new information we should know?"

"No, sir." None except for the Diabetes Scholarship Application screaming from my backpack like the Tell-Tale Heart in Edgar Allen Poe's poem I studied in Freshman Lit. "Nothing new."

On that note, I make an abrupt exit from the kitchen, take a warm shower to wash away the grime from indoor club practice, and hunker down in my room to finish my homework in peace. It's hard to make it too far. As soon as my Chromebook screen lights to life, Matt and Clark yell "Bye, Liv. Love you!" simultaneously—those crazy twins. Pippa and I race down the hall and out the back door for one last Olivia Ovation before they leave to go back to their schools.

Matt gives me an extra pat on the back. "I'm praying for you, Livey-loo. Try not to worry about Vandy. Everything's gonna work out." Why do the smallest things seem to make me so emotional lately? When I nod and brush my palms beneath my eyes to wipe away the pesky moisture leaking from them, he pulls me in again and gives me a quick kiss on the temple. I shiver in my jacket as I watch mom and dad hug them, trade sons to hug the other one, and close their doors. My parents stand beside me as we wave to Matt and Clark from the end of the driveway. They each pull out, one turning right, the other left. The chill of the January air sends us back inside and I head straight to my room for more homework. This house is way too quiet without the twins.

Usually, I'm an academic weapon, but after fifteen rather boring and unproductive minutes at my desk, I tire of the psychology assignment. All hope seems to be lost after I reach for my binder and the diabetes application falls out. I shouldn't do it—I know I shouldn't. My fingers hover over my keys for a bit, then I rush to type in the web address.

There's no harm in looking.

My screen goes to a crisp, clean website with the words "Wonderbrink Foundation" scrolling across the top in fancy cursive font. A pull-down menu on the top left takes me to a page about the scholarship. There's all the same information from the handout, and there's also an interactive map of diabetes support group locations.

Hypothetically, if someone were interested in attending a diabetes support group meeting, that person wouldn't have to have diabetes. Right? They could just check it out. There's a group that meets one town over from Barkley, too. The Sugar Shatterers Society. Interesting...

NO. No, this isn't me.

I close the tab and click on the psychology homework, afraid Vanderbilt's admissions department will somehow know if I don't commit to completing every assignment to the best of my ability. Can't let myself, my family, or Ms. O'Donnell down.

Chapter 2
Sugar Shatterers

Saturday mornings should not start this early. My breath comes out in puffs while I sit in my hand-me-down cute, little silver Honda Accord. The Bluegrass Health Hospital looms large before me, but the golden Vanderbilt Commodore *V* beads hanging from my rearview mirror goad me on.

I scurry across the parking lot and stop in front of the giant revolving front door.

Dang it. I am great at many things, but a revolving door is not one of them.

I cannot allow myself to turn and walk back to my car in defeat. Instead, I lunge toward the revolving door with a determined stride, my eyes locked onto the nearest segment like a sprinter at a starting line. I time my approach, adjust my pace, and attempt to slip inside just as the door rotates.

But of course, that doesn't work.

When my shoulder brushes the edge of the glass panel as I squeeze in, I'm forced to hunch slightly. My hands shoot out and I press them against the glass to push it forward. The revolving door resists for a heartbeat—just enough to break my rhythm—and I stumble, then shuffle with choppy steps to keep the momentum going.

The panels whirr in a deliberate, frustrating circle, so I twist my torso and try to slip out before it can trap me in another loop. With one last burst of energy, I half-jump, half-lunge through the opening as the door spits me out into the lobby.

Did... did anyone see that? If I earned a dollar for every time I lived through an embarrassing, awkward moment, I could more than just attend Vanderbilt, I could buy the whole university.

I brush my hands against my jeans and look around for the information desk, where an elderly lady with bifocals and a gray pixie cut points me in the direction of the diabetes support group. If she saw my struggle, she didn't say, which is beyond merciful and kind. That, or she's an excellent actress who deserves an award for keeping a straight face when she was giving me directions.

Anyway, I follow the benevolent thespian's directions, and two rights after the gift shop, a small post and panel sign that reads "Sugar Shatterers Society" points to a closed door.

I take one last bite of my sweet pandesal I brought from the Reyes Panaderya and toss the to-go bag in the trash can. Mini pep talk time: The key to fitting in is to act like you belong. Deep breath.

"Are you going in or are you just planning on staring at the sign?" I jump, startled by a guy about my age behind me. He's, well, he's not short, but he's only an inch or two above my five foot seven inches.

"It's a nice sign." If I could die from being awkward, death would be imminent. First the revolving door, and now this? A nervous giggle spills out of me. He is incredibly hot. Like, I forgot how to form words for a second *HAWT*. Fitted hat on backward with unruly, dirty blond curls poking out, a hunter green Cadiz High School basketball pullover that makes his hazel eyes shimmer... Me likey.

"You sound like the donkey from *Shrek*," Mystery boy deadpans as he crosses his arms across his broad chest.

Huh?

"I like that sign. That is a nice sign." His impersonation of Eddie Murphy as Donkey is spot on, his voice morphing into a high-pitched, mischievous tone, unlike the annoyance I heard a moment ago. He even tilts his hunky head to the side, much like a real donkey might. If he had big pointy ears and a tail...

He reaches around me to grab the nickel handle and I get a whiff of him. Some hypnotic blend of citrus and herb that's subtle and potentially addictive. "Right. Well, some people believe if a door opens by itself, it could mean you'll have an unwanted visitor."

I blink at him, because... what? "You're kidding, right?"

"Donkey, unless you've got some salt to throw over your shoulder, I absolutely am not." He claims a seat on the right side of the room and, of the eight chairs lining the perimeter of the walls, the only one available is right next to him. I'd say "lucky me," but I don't believe in the stuff like my new friend here. If I did, college would already be paid for.

"I'm Paul." Hot boy offers a strong hand.

"Olivia." We shake and I take my seat. "So, this is my first meeting. What should I expect?"

"You should expect a fancy-schmancy nurse to come in and talk about a different topic every week. How to cope with a cursed pancreas that refuses to make insulin, how to eat boring, bland, low-carb foods, that kind of stuff. Diabetes isn't rocket science, and I have an Omnicom."

A what-a-con-a?

"But my stepmom volun-tells me to come so I can 'connect and talk with other people who have diabetes.'" Paul holds up his fingers in air quotations as he imitates a nasally, high-octave Mom voice. He doesn't strike me as a huge fan of the Sugar Shatterers Society.

"Oh." Silence is intimidating, so I continue my interrogation. "How old were you when you found out you had diabetes? And how did you know?" I resist the overwhelming urge to record his responses on my phone.

Paul squints at me. Is that suspicion in his handsome eyes? Maybe I should calm down with the questions. He clears his throat. "If you listen to my dad, I could get pretty moody as a kid. Not that you'd ever believe it, but according to him, I was a holy terror. My grandma was one of those fancy-schmancy nurses, and when I was eight, I stayed over at her house for the weekend..." He shrugs.

"And?"

"And I had to take a whiz like five times a night. Freaked her out and she made my parents make an appointment with my pediatrician. What about you?"

Ignoring his question, I nod as I commit his answers to memory. "So, you're Type 1?"

"Yeah, mostly only obese people riding down the Hershey Highway with no real self-restraint end up with Type 2."

My jaw goes slack. Whoa. I doubt that's true at all, and hello, majorly offensive.

"Wait." He laughs. "You're Type 2, aren't you? Whoops." At least he has the decency to show some remorse. "I'm sorry. I'm a tactless jerk and didn't mean any of that." His words don't match the lack of sincerity in his smirk. What to make of this new acquaintance?

I scoff at his lack of authenticity, then choke that hypocrisy back when I remember my own duplicity. "No, um–" What exactly *am* I doing here?

"Good morning, everyone." A petite nurse in a medical coat pushes a rolling cart through the back door. Various group attendees greet her in response.

"Why don't we start by sharing this week's sweet success stories and any struggles we can support one another with? We'll go clockwise. And since we have a visitor–" she smiles at me and my face flames– "I'll start by introducing myself. I'm Laura Underwood, a Nurse Practitioner here at Bluegrass Baptist Health. I founded the Sugar Shatterers five years ago when my nephew was diagnosed with Type 1 diabetes. We've met weekly ever since."

I nod, and then I'm lost in blood sugar highs and lows,

foot circulation problems, and hypertension issues. All too soon, it's my turn.

"Hi. I'm Olivia James. I'm here to get a feel for things and–"

"She's here because she thought the sign was pretty." Paul smiles smugly and an older gentleman–balding and wearing glasses–snorts at his interruption.

Oh my gosh.

Nurse Underwood purses her lips. "Let's make sure to help Olivia feel welcome. We'd love to have her come back next week." And I bet she would... if I actually had diabetes.

Paul continues to hijack the rest of my turn. "My name hasn't changed in the last five years, so I'm still Paul Roberts. I'm here because I was cursed with this smokin', rock-hard body that—sadly—can't produce insulin. I understand, though. God couldn't make me perfect; he had to make it fair for the rest of the guys."

The nurse blinks but otherwise gives no reaction, others snicker. I'm guessing she's no stranger to Paul's antics. I, on the other hand, laugh when I'm nervous or uncomfortable, and a giggle escapes. Amber will die when she hears this story... except I can't exactly tell her. The nurse ignores Paul and instead introduces a video about coping mechanisms for emotional challenges often faced by people managing diabetes.

When she flips the light off, Paul leans over and whispers, "Why is everything funnier when you're not supposed to laugh?"

"Shhh..." I hiss, but another treacherous giggle

escapes. He's sitting so close his warm arm is pressing up against mine. Is it hot in here?

Fifteen excruciating minutes and two personal testimonies later, the lights flip back on and my retinas burn in protest. Nurse Underwood wraps up the meeting by distributing low-carb granola bars. I take mine and thank her politely, grab my bag from the back of my chair, then turn to leave.

"Wait." Paul shoves his bar in my hand. "Take mine, Donkey. These things taste like chewy cardboard."

"Just what I always wanted, thank you."

He raises his brow. "Now run, run, as fast you can..." He even uses his hand to gesture me away.

I resist the urge to roll my eyes. "Get out of mah swamp, right?" My retort is rewarded with a gorgeous smile brighter than the sun. Should teeth be that straight and white?

"Ha! Don't step on any cracks on your way out." Ok, wow, this boy is seriously superstitious. "See you next Saturday, Donkey." And I kid you not, he holds up his crossed fingers.

Also, *Donkey?* My skin prickles with unease. I guess one more meeting wouldn't hurt, right?

* * *

Nothing like an indoor soccer match to cap off a weird Saturday. Some girls on my travel team go to CHS, Paul's school, so as we pack up our bags to leave, I decide to ask around. *Don't act suspicious, Liv.* I busy myself by taking off my shin guards and changing from my cleats to my slides. "Do any of you know Paul Roberts? I met him this morning and he's—"

"Deceptively charming?" Meagan snorts. "Yeah, everyone knows Paul." Her voice sounds tired. Hopefully, it's from our hard-earned win.

"I was going to ask if he's always that superstitious. He was kind of intense."

"Oh, that." She visibly relaxes, "Yep, he's been like that for a long time. Once, in fourth grade, he refused to go on a field trip because our teacher opened her umbrella inside while we were waiting for the bus. He stayed back at school and helped the librarian shelve books most of the day."

Something about a little boy too afraid to go on a school trip makes me sad. Poor Paul.

"Does someone have a little crush on Paul?" Meagan wiggles her eyebrows and smiles, her eyes bright.

"Paul who?" Xavier steps up and takes my bag from my shoulder, like always. The other half of the Core Four, Amber and Tyler, are right behind him. "Nice passing, by the way."

"Thanks." I adjust the pre-wrap around my ponytail and wrack my brain to think of an acceptable response. "Um, no crush. I was asking about a guy I met this morning. He's got an... interesting personality." I turn back to Meagan, "Please don't mention I asked."

"Well, let me know if you change your mind." She winks and walks off.

"Paul Roberts?" Xavier rubs his chin.

I whip my gaze to meet his. "Wait, you know him?" Is that a good thing or a bad thing?

"We played rec league basketball together. You probably saw him at some of my games. He's... different."

I wait for Xavier to elaborate, but Amber interrupts, "Where did you say you met him again?"

"I had to run to Bluegrass Baptist Health this morning and I met him there." My cheeks heat from my sin of omission. *Please don't ask why I had to stop by a hospital, and in a different town no less.* Although they'd probably assume it's yet another way to pad my volunteer accolades to impress Vandy's admissions office.

"Olivia, are you blushing? You do have a crush, don't you?" Amber's eyes grow wide. I swore off dating after my ex-boyfriend dumped me the week before prom last year. It was humiliating, and if it weren't for Xavier's pity date, I wouldn't have gone at all. But that jewel toned topaz dress was gorgeous and I had killer shoes, so I refused to miss it. (Thank you again, Mrs. Carlson, for talking some sense into me.)

I roll my eyes. "Please stop. He has a friendly face and some quirky behaviors, that's all."

"Mhmm, sure." Amber shares a look I don't trust with Tyler and my scalp prickles. Xavier, on the other hand, stays quiet on the walk back to his car. We head to Ferrell's for a post-match burger, where I make every effort imaginable to not cross-examine him for information on Paul. Xavier isn't quite his usual laid-back self tonight anyway. But he still eats half my fries, so maybe he's just in a contemplative mood.

"You kids enjoying your weekend?" Mr. Winters' voice draws my gaze to a table two rows over from us, where he's standing to leave, hand-in-hand with his wife. Aww.

"Yes sir." Xavier beams, his happy-go-lucky demeanor shining through again. "Liv here just killed it at her soccer match." *Killed it* is generous, and my face flames at the attention.

"Also, we're at Ferrell's, so life's pretty great at the moment." Amber, for being so petite, can absolutely annihilate some chili cheese fries.

"This is my wife, Charlotte." Mrs. Winters nods hello as Mr. Winters introduces each of us, then asks, "You guys ready for your big basketball game Monday?"

"Hope so. Anything can happen." Tyler says this as if he and Xavier haven't started varsity since freshman year, two of the highest scorers on the team.

Mr. Winters glances at his wife, then back to us. "Well, good luck, and stay out of trouble."

"You too, sir." Xavier grins. Amber, Tyler, and I smile as well, then I get back to my burger. Why is it always a bit bizarre to see teachers outside of school?

Five minutes after he leaves, our waitress delivers four sundaes to our table, courtesy of Mr. Winters. The whipped cream, hot fudge, and cherry help me appreciate a little more why everyone loves him so much. Xavier, of course, ice cream aficionado that he is, is in heaven. Guilt takes some of the joy out of the treat when I think about Paul's "tasteless food" comment. An image of him here with us, a fifth wheel to our Core Four, missing out on such a treat because he likely wouldn't be able to partake in such a decadent dessert.

I need to make good on my promise to "stay out of trouble."

Chapter 3
A Slam Dunk Disaster

Sundays are, by far, my favorite day of the week. First, church. Second, Grace & Glimmer is closed so I don't have to work. Tyler's mom, Mrs. Manning, owns the trendy consignment shop downtown. Third, soccer games are pretty uncommon on Sundays. And finally, the Core Four usually get together for an afternoon movie or to watch a football game.

Not so great about this particular Sunday: the cold. Forget January chill, it was practically a polar vortex when the fam packed into Dad's old mini-van and left for church. We were uncharacteristically late to the service because *winter*. On the bright side, the pews are full despite the weather. Fortunately, my besties saved a seat for me. Unfortunately, we sit near the front in the center aisle, so I can't slip in like the discreet ninja I wish I could pretend to be.

Pastor Reyes continues to preach as I squeeze past Tyler and Amber to slide in beside Xavier. He pats my crazy red curls down when I pull my hat off and tuck my chilly hands inside it on my lap. Hopefully I haven't missed much. I love how beautiful and serene the sanctuary looks after Christmas, and I'm glad they kept the decorations up. Stunning evergreen garland still covers the altar at the front, and soft candles flicker delicately.

I should stop daydreaming and give my attention to the preacher, but when Xavier adjusts to rest his arm on the back of the pew—behind me—I can't help but wonder if he has any idea what that does to a girl. Thank goodness I'm sitting or these weak knees would buckle.

Focus, Liv. Focus on Pastor Reyes.

"Therefore encourage one another and build each other up, just as in fact you are doing." Pastor Reyes clears his throat from behind his wooden podium as he finishes his sermon on 1 Thessalonians 5:11. After the offering, Mr. Manning closes the service in prayer and I give Amber and Xavier's hand a little squeeze when we say "Amen."

Tyler's stomach growls so loud a lady in the pew in front of us turns around, brows high. He merely grins. "So, what are we thinking for lunch today, guys?"

"The Reyes Panaderya!" Amber's wide eyes sparkle with hope.

"Closed on Sundays." Xavier shrugs, and she sags back against the pew.

"Hobby Lobby, Chick-fil-A, and the Reyes Panaderya." Amber grumbles. "All the places I want to go on a Sunday." She grabs her bag and we file out of the pew to make our way from the sanctuary to the parking lot.

"We're going to my house. You can eat the same food." Xavier raises a brow, head tilted.

Amber laughs. "It's not the same!" Did I mention she's passionate about food?

"My mom has a giant pot of adobo calling your name. I'll even put on an apron if it makes a difference." Xavier smirks at Amber. We all know she's a huge sucker for Mrs. Reyes' adobo. Who isn't?

"We do look cute in those aprons," Tyler quips. He's never been one to lack confidence.

"Will you wrap my silverware in one of the fancy napkin things?"

"Don't push your luck." Xavier turns to me and gives my knitted purple beanie a tug. "Need a ride?"

He pulls my hat down so far, I have to lift my face to peek at him. "Yes, please." My words come out in a little puff of white. Thank goodness Xavier's car has seat heaters. Xavier's house is halfway between my house and the church, so it's a short ride, but not so short that I can't appreciate having my tush toasted.

Xavier lives in a duplex connected to his family's restaurant and it's one of the coolest set-ups. Friends and family enter the Reyes house from the back entrance, where one can either walk straight into the adjoining kitchen, or turn right and enter the living space. After the four of us stuff our faces with the delicious chicken dish, much to Mrs. Reyes' delight, we file up the stairs to Xavier's rec room. The corkscrew stairs are my favorite, but there's no doubt I'd weigh six-hundred pounds if I lived that close to the panaderya.

We reach the top of the stairs, and when the caddy

cornered couches come into view, Amber, Tyler and I race for the stack of pillows and blankets. The goal? Stake claim to the tortilla blanket, a circle of warmth that looks like a giant piece of flatbread. It's like winning the middle cinnamon roll when Mom pulls the pan out of the oven. If you get that, you're someone special.

No surprise that Tyler, all six feet of him, launches himself on top of it before either Amber or I can get within a yard of the thing. And since they're a giant mushfest, he and Amber share the dang thing. I sit to the left of the happy couple, snuggled up in a massive, colorful blanket with Xavier's sisters faces covering the front. It was a gag-gift to their parent's last Christmas, but at least it's warm. Xavier's stretched out to their right, sans blanket, and the boys win this afternoon—we're watching football.

At least the Commanders win.

* * *

Monday is a drag. I have one pop quiz, zero TikTok disruptions, and a substitute teacher in calculus, so if nothing else, I can play on my phone a little during last period. Texts start pouring in from a number I don't recognize.

> Unknown number: DONKEY! Home basketball game tonight at 7. You comin'?

What in the what?

> Me: 'Scuse me? Who is this?

> Unknown number: Your favorite ogre, Paul. This is known as an "invitation." I have a basketball game tonight at 7 PM, Central Standard Time, Monday, January 21, in the year of our Lord, Cadiz High School gymnasium. Your presence is requested as you will serve as my good luck charm this evening.

He would say that. Did Meagan give him my number? And who texts like that?

> Me: How did you get this number, ogre?

> Paul: Luck. ;)

> Me: *eyeroll* No such thing.

> Paul: *SCOFF* Skeptic donkey. I bet you don't believe in Bigfoot, either. So… you coming?

Cue the dull ache in my chest. I can't keep waiting for Xavier to give some indication he feels the same way I do about him, as something more than platonic best friends. Some lingering glance, actual words like "I AM IN LOVE WITH YOU, LIV…" Wouldn't that be nice, amiright? Might as well dive right in.

> Me: If you promise not to call me Donkey, I'll try my best to be there.

He responds with a thumbs up, a four-leaf clover, and

the shocked face emoji. I halfway wonder if he'll uninvite me for dissing superstitions. Maybe I can watch part of Xavier and Tyler's game, then make it to Paul's, too?

* * *

The Barkley Bobcats have been stale for most of the first half. They're down three to Henderson County with two minutes to go in the quarter. Xavier's starting to heat up though, and when he hits a three despite the hands waving in his face, the crowd erupts. I glance at my phone to check the time, then jerk my gaze away in time to see the net swoosh after I miss Xavier's heat check from two feet behind the three-point line. I can't believe he made that.

"Got someplace to be?" Amber motions to my screen. Ok, fine, I'm a little distracted. I need to leave by 7:00 PM to make it to Paul's game in time to catch the second half.

"I have to leave at the half." Which is now a mere thirty seconds away. "I'm going to go ahead and leave so I can let my car warm up."

"I thought you didn't have club soccer on Mondays?" Her face scrunches.

"I don't," I mumble into her hair as I give her a big hug, then reach for my bag.

I turn away as she asks, "Where did you say you had to go?" But I pretend I don't hear her over the rowdy crowd.

Twenty minutes and zero revolving doors later, I reach my destination.

The Cadiz gym is larger than Barkley's. Older, too. It's a standalone building to the right of the school, with a large "Home of the Cadiz Colonels!" in bold, green hand-painted letters above the entrance. I make my way inside and stand by the doors instead of trying to mingle with so many foreign faces filling the wooden bleachers. The scoreboard reveals a close game, much more intense than the one I just left. And it's LOUD. Cheerleaders, the occasional whistle, the pep band blaring, and sneakers squeaking on the court all compete for my attention.

The scoreboard buzzer indicates the end of the third quarter and the teams return to their benches. I locate Paul in the huddle. He's fiddling with the diabetes monitor on his arm and frowns, but his face brightens when he looks up and meets my eyes. He gives a mini-fist pump and mouths "Donkey!" Two of his teammates look over and I watch as their eyebrows raise, their curiosity piqued by my unfamiliar face.

The game starts again, and I can tell by the way Paul passes, dribbles, shoots, everything, that he's good. He's energized and focused, with smooth assists and his ability to bank in easy lay-ups. He's *really* good.

Until he's not.

He looks like he wants to pass the ball, but then he seems confused, a blank look on his face. The other team steals the ball and he's sluggish on his return down the court. He gets the ball back but freezes for a second, disoriented, and gets called for walking. His coach must notice he's off too, because he walks stiffly toward the bench, face ashen, and signals for a timeout. His team-mates and the other players walk back over to their benches, some of their faces pale as well, and not from over-exerting themselves. A nurse from the center table grabs a first aid kit and rushes to Paul's side.

The gym, so hyped-up only moments ago, grows quiet. The crowd watches with anxious expressions, a soft rumble of quiet murmurs. Some spectators bite their nails and others clutch their neighbors' hands. Tense whispers of "hypoglycemic" and "low blood sugar" swirl around me.

The nurse rips open a gel packet and helps squeeze it into Paul's mouth. An eternity seems to pass before the color returns to his face and he appears himself again. The coach pats him on the back as he stays glued to the bench, the nurse remaining in the seat beside him. The crowd breathes a collective sigh of relief and claps politely when the coach speaks to the ref, nodding his head with intense animation as the players walk back to their positions on the court.

The game resumes, played to a much more somber, yet relieved, group of fans. I continue to watch as the nurse scolds and fusses over Paul. My ears grow hot when he notices me watching and winks. Of course, he does. At least his juvenile gesture slows my rapid heart. A little tension drains from my shoulders as well.

Paul sits on the bench the remainder of the game, slowly gaining energy by whatever was in that little packet the nurse shoved down his throat. He cheers for his teammates, but he never does go back in the game. When the final buzzer sounds, the Colonels barely squeak out a victory, but at least they still won. I stay put in my little spot by the wall trying to figure out my next move. Do I stay and say hi? Give him a little wave and slip off, no big deal? Should I have brought a wing woman?

Mercifully, Paul leaves the post-game huddle as it disperses and walks straight over to me. He stops about three feet from me and, *hello* biceps.

Chill, brain. This may be a strictly platonic thing here.

Then he offers me a lazy grin and I lose my mind again. "Donkey, thought you'd chickened out on me."

"And here I thought you might regret inviting me. Some good luck charm I am, huh?" Diabetes must be a difficult disease to manage.

"Psh. We won, didn't we? Don't tell me you're worried about my low blood sugar. My pancreas never works." He dismisses my worry as if he didn't just have to sit out the entire fourth quarter. When I get home, I'm shredding that stupid Wonderbrink application.

"Is something wrong with your monitor?"

He shrugs. "Sensor detached right before half-time. I guess it wasn't reading right. The nurse helped and said it might need recalibration."

Um, that seems important. "Well, glad you were able to cheer for your teammates. And you recovered quite nicely."

Oh geez. My cheeks may burst into flames. No telling how he might interpret *that* statement.

Which is not at all, since he stops paying attention to me altogether as the dance team walks by, a long line of mid-drifts calling his name.

"Later, Donkey."

Later, Donkey? Is he serious right now? Do you know the word used to describe a person who left their best friend's game, drove the better part of half-an-hour, to be dismissed for the lure of bare bellybuttons?

Miffed. If there's a better word for embarrassed and annoyed, then that's the word I'm looking for.

* * *

At lunch on Tuesday, Tyler and Xavier recap what turned out to be an intense game, hard-won in overtime.

I lower my fork. "You scored thirty points?" I'm impressed.

"Don't act so surprised." He tugs on my mass of a ponytail but then stops abruptly "Wait, why are you surprised? Weren't you there?"

"Yes, but..."

He raises his brows.

"...I left at the half."

He stares, his face expressionless. "Why?"

"Um," best to stick with the truth here, "Paul texted me and invited me to his game."

For a moment, he says nothing. Then, "Geez, Liv, all the way in Cadiz? Why didn't you say something at school?" Xavier's cheeks flush. What's he so worked up about? I look to Amber and Tyler to see if they're as weirded out as I am, but they're no longer paying much attention to us.

"Why is this such a big deal? He texted me in sixth period and I didn't see you before tipoff."

He crosses his arms. "Did you forget how to text?"

Whoa.

"Did you forget how to chill?" I scoot back from my seat across the table and pull my lunch tray closer. "I didn't know I needed your permission." All my muscles decide to go a little rigid and I stare at him, stiff as can be. We don't fight and I don't like it. At all. My outburst gains the attention of the rest of our table.

Xavier blinks, then his face softens and his broad shoulders fall from his ears. "Of course you don't. Sorry. I've never scored that many points in a game and I was excited. You're usually there cheering for me. We gas each other up."

My ramrod straight back loosens as I exhale, because he's right. We always cheer for each other. We support Amber at her dance recitals, Xavier and Tyler at basketball, football, and whatever other season they're in, and me at soccer. Always. I swallow my guilt. "I'm sorry, too." I hate that my voice comes out in a whisper.

"So, are you talking to Paul?" Xavier asks, his face again hard to read.

"Oh my gosh, are you?" Amber's suddenly *very* interested in our conversation. I knew she was listening.

"What? No! I just went to his game. He's crazy superstitious and said I'd bring him good luck."

"Barf. And did you?" Xavier's jaw tenses.

What the heck? Can he see the frown I feel taking over my face? "He had a diabetic emergency at the start of the fourth quarter. It was kind of scary."

Amber's eyes widen as she covers her mouth and Tyler whispers, "Geez."

Xavier's mouth falls open, but he recovers quickly

and mumbles, "Guess you're not the good luck charm he thought you'd be."

"Xavier!" Amber scoffs. Tyler has the good sense to look away, scratching a phantom itch on his neck.

"*Luckily,*" I grit through my teeth, "his coach recognized what was happening and called a time-out. The nurse helped him and he spent the end of the game on the bench."

When Xavier rolls his eyes, Amber calls him out on it. "Xavier, if I didn't know better, I'd say someone is a little jealous."

"Of Paul? Please. I just thought we were there for each other. We encourage each other."

Did he just quote his dad's sermon against me? There's no way Xavier's jealous. No way.

"We'll let you guys have a moment," Tyler stacks Amber's tray on top of his, then reaches for her hand as they walk to the kitchen conveyor belt to drop them off. I stare at their backs as they walk across the tiled floor.

"Look, Liv. It's just... it felt like you ditched us for some guy you barely know. It's weird, that's all."

I tug at the strings on his hoodie. "Stop pouting, silly. You're still my number one."

"I'm not pouting. I'm just protective." He puffs his chest out.

"You never pout? What about that time the Dairy Dip ran out of mint chocolate chip ice cream."

His puffed-up chest deflates. "That was one of the saddest days of my life."

Yep, he's back and life is good again. Although, life

was a little better when I thought, even if it was only for a second, that Xavier may have been even a teensy bit jealous.

Wishful thinking.

Chapter 4
Alley OOPS

Working at an upscale consignment shop has its ups and downs. Cons: Occasionally, a snooty patron will try to sell their clothes, and they'll inevitably get their panties in a wad when Grace & Glimmer doesn't offer a ridiculous, unreasonable amount of money for their second-hand clothes.

Well, no ma'am, we don't want your thread-bare, stretched out sweater with pit stains. How dare we?

Or a popular classmate from school will sell us something awesome that I could never pay retail for, but I tend to pass on despite my employee discount, because how awkward would it be to wear a super rare, impeccable half-zip Lululemon hoodie in vivid plum? Please. I don't need to advertise that I'm a plebian.

Pro: Besides having first dibs at new inventory and said employee discount, the boss is Tyler's mom, and she tries to be flexible with soccer and school obligations when she schedules my hours. She's generous when I need extra hours—I always need extra hours—and on rare slow nights, it's nice to squeeze in some homework. Plus, there's usually a steady flow of friends from school who come into the shop, and that helps pass the time.

Like tonight. Amber's here, and she brought salted caramel hot chocolate, too. She's searching through the clearance shoes while I tag coats and jackets.

"Did you hear that Jasmine Garcia was accepted early decision to Transylvania?" Amber places a suede wedge back on the rack and pulls out her phone. "She posted on Instagram."

Tag.

"Think she'll swim there? I bet she'd kill it in DIII." I am really in a rhythm with this tag gun...

Tag.

"Dunno. Uh, everything ok? You just tagged the same coat twice."

Dangit.

"Yeah, sorry. Just anxious about Vandy, I guess."

Next coat. Tag.

"Talk to Xavier since school?"

"Nope." Another new coat. Tag.

"He was pretty upset at lunch, huh?" Amber asks as she takes a sip from her hot chocolate and raises her brows.

"I didn't realize how severe my treachery was by going to Paul's game, but I get the impression my true offense was not coming out directly and saying, 'I'm going to my friend Paul's game tonight.'"

"No silly, you have every right to go anywhere you want, but why didn't you just tell us you were going to your friend Paul's game last night instead?"

Because I met him under sketchy circumstances and Xavier will never see me as more than his best friend. Except I don't say that. Instead, I say, "Yeah, you're right, and I'm sorry. I told Xavier basically the same thing once you guys left."

But I guess I see their point. Mom once told me if you have to hide something, you probably know it's not the best decision.

"So, Paul, huh?" Amber waggles her eyebrows and I accidentally retag a fourth coat, causing both of us to fall in a ridiculous fit of giggles. Maybe having friends visit during working hours isn't all that productive.

Mrs. Manning steps out from the back and takes in my tagging catastrophe. Amber diverts her gaze, but I spy her grin before she turns her attention back to the shoes. "Well girls, it's a slow night, and there must be something wrong with the tagging gun." She picks it up and shakes it, and all three of us giggle.

We toss our empty hot chocolate cups and Amber helps me hang the coats on the circular rack.

"Amber, I have no idea about Paul. I mean, I met him Saturday."

"I get it, but... what about Xav—"

"Don't. Please." I shake my head but relax when Amber purses her lips together and it's clear she won't push the issue further.

"Fine, fine." She hangs the last coat and tucks her phone in her coat pocket. "I better get out of here or I'll be late for dance."

After Amber leaves, I still have an hour of work left. It's turned into a rather slow night, and I can't shake the idea that my friends are still disappointed. I'd probably feel the same way if one of them left a soccer game. Especially one where I played lights out. I will fix this in my own special way–with a personalized cartoon apology.

I grab an outdated sales flyer from beneath the front counter and flip it over to the blank side, then draw myself crying giant tears that flood the bottom of the paper in a deep blue pool of water. My cartoon self is wearing a shirt that says, "Alley OOPS," with alley marked out and "Sorry" written over the top of it. The Os are basketballs.

Mrs. Manning starts to flip the back lights off. "Go ahead and close up, Olivia. The weather app on my phone says we're under a winter weather advisory. Looks like we won't be getting any more customers tonight."

"Yes ma'am." I snap a picture of the cartoon in my binder, send the image to the Core Four, and close out the drawer. I tell Mrs. Manning goodnight, then slip out into the chilly parking lot.

Wednesday morning, I wake up to several texts.

Barkley Public Schools: No school today due to inclement weather; this will be a traditional snow day. Stay warm.

Yessss....

Paul: Oi, Donkey. Did ye get a snow day?

Me: Ogre, I did. I love the snow. It's like a big ol' playground! I'm probably gonna hang out with some buddies and drink hot chocolate. You?

Paul: Way to rub it in. We still have classes online so I'm stuck in my swamp. I knew I should have put a spoon under my pillow.

Me: Oof.

Also, he should have done *what?*

Core Four Group Chat: (Three heart notifications pop up on the cartoon image I shared last night.)

Awwww... I rest my head back on my pillow and hold the phone above me to continue reading.

Xavier to the Core Four Group Chat: You guys want to stop by the Pandereya for lunch? Everyone think they can get here ok?

The salt/scraper truck rolls by as I finish reading his text. That's an affirmative. I know Amber wouldn't miss the chance at good food, and Tyler wouldn't miss the chance to be with her. We all text back "yes" to meeting at noon. And then because I'm me, my phone slips and hits me on the chin.

Ouch.

I conquer a small mountain of homework until Pippa gets the zoomies around eleven o'clock, so I leash her up and fold the cartoon into my pocket. I keep a tight grip on her leash as we walk to the Reyes' Panaderya on the corner of Maple and Main. Warm, inviting lights spill out onto the sidewalk and I pull my jacket tighter around me. This thick coat is a big brother hand-me-down (a.k.a. Clark Couture), which is nice, since late January in Kentucky is colder than a snowman's hug in a walk-in freezer.

"Come on, Pippa. We can do this." My voice is low but she wags her tail in response. I guide her around the side of the building and enter through the back door. The little bell above it chimes softly, and I wait to hand off Pippa's leash to Xavier's little sister. Jasmine loves Pippa's field-trips and usually takes her to their upstairs apartment for a play date with the Reyes' golden lab.

As I wait near the kitchen, I'm greeted by the familiar smell of vinegar and soy sauce–Mrs. Reyes' delicious adobo waiting to come together. One quick peek through the swinging kitchen door and I see that the restaurant is bustling with the lunch crowd. I spot Xavier clearing a table near the back. He notices me, and I melt a little when he smiles and walks toward us.

"Hey, buddy." Xavier reaches down to scratch behind Pippa's ear. Pippa melts like butter around him. With his easy-going manner, relief washes over me. "Did you walk here? It's freezing."

"Yeah, well, my legs work fine and gas isn't free." My legs are stiff from the cold, but petrol costs a pretty penny, so here I stand with my pupsicle. "I thought I'd bring my best girl around for support." Pippa's big brown eyes seem to offer encouragement.

"Always good to have Pippa around," Xavier agrees, straightening to meet my gaze, when we're interrupted by Jasmine. We're silent as she fawns over Pippa. Once she's taken her up the stairs, he asks, "You're early. What's up?"

I bite my bottom lip, trying my best to ignore the guilt in my stomach. "Not to beat a dead horse, but I was kind of hoping we could talk about Monday a little more."

Xavier's eyebrows arch. "Nah, no big deal that you bailed. I only scored thirty points."

"Xavier Reyes!" I whack him in the chest with the back of my hand. "Seriously, I'm sorry. I know I should've been there, but—"

"But you were too busy watching Paul Roberts in another county," Xavier finishes for me, his tone light yet laced with sarcasm.

I sink into the seat by the staff lockers and rest my head against the wall behind me, shoulders slumped. "Okay, I deserve that. But it wasn't about Paul. Fine, maybe a little." Xavier's not stupid. "But mostly, it was because I made a selfish decision when I bailed and didn't tell you. I should've been supporting my best friend."

Xavier's expression softens. "Yeah, I wish you had been."

"But according to the universal best friend code, we're also supposed to be happy for each other when something good happens. Being invited to a social function because a guy *might* like me–and I'm really stressing the *might* part here–isn't that a good thing?"

Maybe I imagine it, maybe it's wishful thinking, but

I swear I see Xavier's jaw tighten before he rubs his hand against the back of his neck. Hard to know for sure since he's staring at the floor. "Yeah, that's a good thing."

I nudge him with my knee. "I mean, what's not to love, right?"

He snorts, then rolls his eyes.

"Hey!" I laugh. I lift my head from the wall and glance at him. A smile tugs at my lips. "You were amazing, right? Scored the winning shot, too, I hear?"

The last remnant of his frown finally melts away, a grin breaking through. "You bet I did. The crowd went insane."

"I'm sure they did." I unroll my artwork and hand him the cardstock drawing like a preschooler gifting their mom with their morning table work. "Here, you should keep this." When he studies it close and grins, my shoulders relax.

"How'd you make this so fast? This is amazing." It's always a bit nerve-wracking when someone inspects my art, so I duck my head and turn away. I look up to see Xavier grab tape and then hang it inside his work locker. He rubs his free hand along his jawline.

"Look, Liv, I get it. I guess Paul's a big deal to you. And it's not like we're not allowed to have friends outside of the Core Four." I stare at his face, waiting for him to continue. "But you're a big deal to me." His voice is low and his eyes are focused on the ground.

Someone tell my fluttering heart to calm down. I mask the treacherous blush that I can feel warming my face with what I pray looks like a teasing grin. "Aww,

Xavier, you mean to tell me you have a heart under all that tough-guy exterior?"

He slides down in the seat next to me and bumps my shoulder with his. "Let's not get carried away, Liv. I'm trying to apologize for overreacting. I might have. A little."

I let that go and rest my head on his shoulder with easy familiarity. "So, we're good?"

He gives me a ridiculous, dramatic sigh. Xavier would make a terrible actor. "I suppose I can forgive you. But only if you promise to come to my next game."

"Duh. Unless I have soccer, or Amber has—"

"And maybe bring a pint of cookie dough ice cream."

"Fine. I'll even throw in some warm brownies, just for you."

"Now you're talking."

There's a comfortable silence, and then Xavier clears his throat. "So... Paul, huh?"

I remove my head from his shoulder and place my chin in my hands, elbows on my knees. "Um, no. Yes? I don't know. He's... charming? Eccentric? I've never met anyone quite like him."

Xavier snorts. He's become an exceptional snorter of late.

"I don't know what to think about all his superstitions." Not to mention the false pretenses of our friendship. It was cleansing to shred that Wonderbrink application after the game Monday night. It's now in the bottom of my trashcan in one million tiny pieces.

But do I *like* like Paul? I've nursed an intense crush on Xavier since freshman year, but when I confided in

Amber, we both thought he would be one hundred percent freaked out. I convinced myself it would ruin our friendship if our feelings weren't mutual. Or worse, we dated but then had a nasty, dramatic breakup.

No, thank you.

I only told Pippa and Jesus that my crush never died, but I merely subdued it, and I've been in love with him since. No one needs to know that, for the same reasons I never said anything after ninth grade.

Paul, though? It's complicated.

The silent spell is broken when Tyler and Amber tumble in through the back door, stomping their boots free of snow on the entrance mat.

"I'm going to need something extra spicy today. My whole body is numb." She shivers out of her coat and gloves, and we all hang our outerwear on the hooks next to the back locker.

We enjoy an intensely spicy lunch and waste away the afternoon in Xavier's rec room. This time, Amber gets the tortilla blanket, but I get double dog cuddles when Pippa and the Reyes' Weimaraner, Multo, snuggle in on both my sides.

Snow days are the best.

Tyler places his empty bowl of popcorn on the coffee table. "'Bout time to get ready for church."

"You want a ride to youth group?" Xavier taps my toe with the end of his.

"Yes, please. But can I have a bowl of adobo first?" Or some hot Sinigang? Just feed me and tell my dog she's a good girl. We grab our belongings and start the long, arduous process of dressing to go out in a mild blizzard.

Xavier leaves for a few minutes while I retrieve Pippa and he returns with a to-go box. He pulls on his navy fleece, grabs his keys, kisses his mom on the cheek, and takes Pippa's leash.

When all is well with my best friends, all is well in life. My secret, unrequited crush out of mind.

Sort of.

* * *

The next best thing to school being cancelled is a delay, which is what I wake up to Thursday. Kind of a bummer that there's no new scholarship information in Mrs. Carlson's office when I stop by before first period, but I get another sticky note from Xavier in fourth. This one has an *O* in the center with the number seven in the top left corner.

A mechanical pencil is my only option for a medium, but I draw eight gnarly tentacles coming from the sides of the letter, complete with detailed suction cups. I give him a friendly face and write "Ink-credible" around him in cutesy hand-lettering. He's adorable.

Tyler glances over my shoulder and takes a look. "That'd be cooler if it had ink shooting out of its butt."

"I think it's tenta-cool." Amber's face spreads into a wide grin. She's clearly proud of her punny joke. Xavier rolls his eyes and I tuck the sticky into my notebook as the bell rings. The cephalopod makes a great neighbor to the blue sticky note snowman.

Mom's acting weird in the kitchen when I get home from soccer. She's not her usual chatty self. She doesn't say a word and when she starts humming, I lean over my homework sprawled out on the table in front of me and peer at her, curious.

"What?" Her voice is unnaturally high, and she's failing miserably to hide a smile behind the dishes she unloads from the dishwasher.

"I didn't say anything." I close my Chromebook and narrow my eyes at her odd behavior.

"Oh, well, there might be some mail for you. I put it on your desk."

Might be some mail? My spine straightens at the funny feeling in my tummy. I jump up and run down the hall, Pippa hot on my heels, and screech to a halt in front of the tiny desk in my teal bedroom. I stare, frozen, at the large (*large!*) packet on my desk. Pippa must sense my trepidation because she lets out a whimper beside me, her tail wagging.

I wrench myself out of my daze and rip open the thick seal.

"Read it!" I hadn't even heard Mom and Dad follow me into my room. Deep breath...

Dear Miss Olivia James,

Congratulations! On behalf of the Admissions Committee, it is my pleasure to offer you admission to Vanderbilt University's Class of...

I don't get past the first full sentence. Instead, I clutch the paper to my chest and squeeze the life out of that sucker. It takes less than a millisecond before the screaming starts.

"Ahhhhhhhhhh!" Mom, Dad, and I squeal at a crazy high decibel. We bounce and laugh like hyenas hyped up on Red Bull. Pippa does her best to bark over our ruckus, and when we finally stop, my parents' eyes are glistening. We squeeze into a massive hug. We're the living embodiment of the octopus I drew earlier—arms are everywhere.

Dad muffles into my hair. "We're so proud of you."

"We knew you'd get in, no doubts at all," Mom reassures me.

After we compose ourselves, we Facetime with Matt and Clark, and then once I've showered and finished my homework, I Facetime Xavier, Tyler, and Amber. I've replayed this moment in my mind thousands of times, and it's surreal that I finally get to tell my best friends my big news.

"Hey guys, I have something important to tell you." I hate how my voice trembles with nerves.

Xavier's smile falters a little and his eyebrows draw together.

"Everything ok?" Amber asks.

"So much better than ok. I got an acceptance letter from Vandy this afternoon." If my face could split apart from happiness, I'd need some super glue right now.

Tyler mumbles something like, "Duh."

"Of course you did! We're so proud of you." Amber squeals.

Xavier's signature heartthrob grin smiles back at me from the screen. "That's incredible, Liv. I'm not surprised, but I am proud of you. You're one of the smartest, most determined people I know. They're lucky to have you."

"Thanks guys." I can feel my cheeks warm at their praise.

"I'm serious, Liv. You're going to do amazing things there." He fixes his gaze on me and I forget to breathe for a minute.

"Ahem," Amber mumbles, breaking up the moment. "Well, seriously, this is a huge deal, Liv. We need to celebrate."

"Yes!" Xavier and Tyler respond at the same time, probably because Core Four celebrations usually involve ice cream.

"How about Ferrel's on Sunday after church, and then the Commodore gets to pick the movie?" I'll take Ferrel's any day, so we agree to Amber's plan.

"I'll bring the ice cream," Xavier shares as we say our goodbyes. Of course he will.

Should I text Paul? Would that be weird? Meh, why not?

> Me: Ogre! Guess what?

> Paul: Chicken butt?

Why is that always funny to me?

> Me: I got accepted to Vandy today.

> Paul: That's great, Donkey. In the mornin', I'm makin' waffles.

> Me: Uhhh, ok. ???

> Paul: Sheesh, have you even watched Shrek? Amateur.

> Me: Oooohhh, right!… and I thought the Waffle Fairy was just a bedtime story!

Paul: Better. Nice job, Commodore Donkey.

Me: Thanks. :)

I wait for Paul to continue the thread, but he's gone quiet.

I return to my acceptance materials to find there's also a roommate questionnaire—fun—and a separate flier with information about their arts program.

DROOL.

Tonight feels like my birthday and Christmas, all at the same time.

When I've sorted through the rest of the information, I grab the acceptance letter and read the last paragraph.

"...To accept your offer of admission, please log in to your MyAppVU portal and submit your enrollment deposit by the deadline indicated. Additionally, you will find information regarding housing, orientation, and other important next steps to prepare for your arrival on campus."

Oooh, more fun? Yes, please.

I open my Chromebook, follow the instructions for the MyAppVU portal, and lose myself in the abundance of all things Vanderbilt. Then I click on the Funding pull-down menu with options to learn more about scholarships and grants, all of which I'm already well-versed in, and finally, my personalized financial aid package. I bite my bottom lip and shake out my hands, hesitant to click the link that could very well put a real damper on the evening. I press down on the keypad and watch as the "Student's Expected Contribution" page loads with a number so massive it makes my head spin—so, so many zeros.

The acceptance paper I'd clutched so dearly a mere half-hour ago drops to the floor, right along with my jaw.

Pippa pulls me out of my stupor by licking my hand, and when I look at my phone again, there's a text from Xavier.

> Xavier: ATTA GIRL! PROUD OF YOU, LIV!

I lay my head on my desk with a resounding thunk. Pippa whimpers and rests her chin on my lap.

This is much worse than I expected.

So, so much worse.

Chapter 5
Movies & Mental Meltdowns

"**D**onkey, you made it." Paul deadpans from his chair, waving lack-luster jazz-hands before interlocking his fingers on his stomach. His long legs sprawl out in front of him. "Figured after you got accepted to Vandy you'd consider yourself too good for us Sugar Shatterers." He's got his hat on backward again, and wisps of blond locks peek out, hanging in damp curls, perhaps from a recent shower.

"Happy to see me, Paul?" I fake a yawn to feign disinterest. Feign, because man, it's hard to look away.

"That's what I said, ain't it?" He pats the seat next to him. "We ogres are like onions, Donkey. Just 'cause I didn't squeal like a little girl and jump up to swallow you in a bear hug doesn't mean I'm not glad you're here."

Now that I know what I'm missing, I slump down into the seat. His lack of a similar, excited greeting is a bit disappointing. Also, what am I doing here? Again. Did I come for Paul, or because that Wonderbrink scholarship is suddenly *much* more appealing?

Yes.

I consider his droopy shoulders. "Are *you* glad to be here?"

"Meh. Stepmom made me come." He closes his eyes and I take the opportunity to stare at his long lashes. How unfair that a boy should be blessed with those when I'd be hard-pressed to find a false set like his, and even if I did, I'd probably glue my eyelids shut upon application.

"Do you get to see your mom much?"

He opens one eye to consider my question, then shrugs and closes it again. "Tuesdays, Thursdays, and every other weekend."

"Are you close to either of your parents?" Or is it "any" of your parents? How do stepparents fit into the equation? My family is so close, it's impossible to imagine them apart, or having to divide my time between them.

"Are you always so nosy, Donkey?"

"Guilty, and—"

And we'll have to save the relationship calculus for another time because Nurse Underwood just entered the now-full room.

"Good morning, everyone. I have big news for our Sugar Shatterers." Nurse Underwood's face glows with excitement, her grin wide. She clasps her hands together and makes a point to look around at each of us. "I'm happy to announce the First Annual Sugar Shatterers Walk for a Cure. This special fundraiser will allow us to raise public awareness about the importance of a healthy lifestyle in preventing and controlling diabetes."

"*Walk* for a cure? Where's the urgency in that? Seems like it might be more appropriate for people to run." Paul holds his hands out as if to ask, *Isn't that obvious?*

"Paul, I'm so glad you're paying attention. Many people don't realize diabetes is such a serious disease."

"If it weren't, wouldn't we call it *LIVE*abetes."

Can eyes actually pop out of their sockets? Is that a legit worry I should have? He did not just say that.

"Funny." Except based on Nurse Underwood's pinched expression, I'd guess she's more annoyed than amused, her lips pressed thin. She recovers quickly and a smile replaces her grimace. "The walk will be announced on the Bluegrass Baptist Health social media channels and the hospital website later this week. In addition to our regularly scheduled meetings, those interested in volunteering can plan to stick around for an extra thirty minutes after each of our next six to eight meetings."

Ooooh, organizing things, always fun for me. Art *and* something semi-athletic? Yes, please. And I wonder if Nurse Underwood would let me design the flyers. While she leads the rest of the meeting, most of my time is spent mentally planning. I could do a graffiti-esque poster. Something whimsical and fun. Or maybe something nature-inspired since the walk will be outside. My insides are vibrating—let me wipe the drool off my chin.

Paul, though, merely yawns and begins a rather unhurried exit. He twirls his car keys around his finger. "Later, Donkey."

"You're not staying to help plan the walk?" I bite my bottom lip. *Please stay.*

"Nay lass. Fun for you, maybe, but not for this ogre.

Count me out." He salutes me (salutes!) and then, he's off.

Alrighty.

The rest of Saturday is a big distraction. Nurse Underwood agreed to let me design flyers and a logo (and I resisted the urge to hug her) so I plan to spend most of the afternoon at my desk, sketching.

"Whatcha workin' on, hun?" Mom places a stack of clean clothes on the foot of my bed, then stands behind me as I work.

"Umm..." I cling to my flair pen so mom won't notice my fingers twitch. "A friend told me about the First Annual Sugar Shatterers Walk for a Cure and they're in need of promotional materials. I offered to create some sample flyers and a logo, but they need them ASAP so they can announce the event."

"That sounds right up your alley. What friend did you say?"

"Paul Roberts. He goes to school with Meagan from soccer. He's kind of goofy and he's in the diabetes support group organizing the walk."

"Well, how nice. Those look great. Maybe the family could participate in the walk?" She picks up a draft of the flyer. "Cadiz? I guess your art reputation has made the rounds. How about that!"

Uh, not exactly.

She kisses the top of my head. "You've got soccer in half an hour. Time get away from you?"

One quick glance at the clock and... whoa. It really did. I hurry to put the finishing touches on the letters in "Sugar" and start cleaning up my workspace.

I'm putting the flair pens in their container when Mom reaches over to adjust the acceptance letter hung proudly on the cork board above my desk. She squeezes my shoulder. Yep, there they are. Those sinking feelings of dread and guilt I'd forgotten to pay mind to while I sketched are back with a vengeance. The tight feeling in my chest isn't what I'd call fun, either.

* * *

When I get to the indoor center, there are orange cones lined up all over the field. Looks like today is a drill day. Normally, I'd prefer a scrimmage, but repetitiveness is fine by me. My mind is elsewhere.

Warm-ups are nice too because I can run out the soreness in my back from sitting hunched over my art all afternoon. My first station is dribbling, and every time I round a cone, I have a new terrible thought. Cone one: I kick the ball a little too hard, angry that, despite my talents and hard work, without more scholarships, I definitely won't be able to go to Vandy. Cone two: I'm more careful not to over kick the ball, but a heavy sense of sadness washes over me as my dreams of following in O'Connell's footsteps slip away. Cone three: Ugh, the injustice of it all. Socio-economic classes are totally unfair. Cone four: Why am I not good enough? Cone five: Ok, this is toxic. Maybe I should try to work out complex math problems instead. Cone six: Must channel my emotions into practice. Cone seven: But other kids with GPAs lower than mine get to go to their dream schools. Cone eight: Ok, lying is bad and the Wonderbrink scholarship is a no–go... How can I reevaluate my future? Cone nine: Oh gosh, what will I do if I can't go to Vandy? Cone ten: I really need to derail this pity-party train and focus on more optimistic thoughts, but instead, I trip over my own foot and wipe out, Beckham style.

Coach Lonnie's loud whistle pierces through the facility, bouncing off the side walls. I grab my left tush cheek and moan.

"Olivia James, what is wrong with you? This is a basic dribbling drill and you're a *senior*. Get your head in the game."

I roll onto my side. "I'm fine, thanks for asking." I am not fine—I accidentally fractured my feelings.

"What? You break your butt?" He grabs me by the elbow and helps me to my feet. My answer depends on who's asking: my uncle or Coach Lonnie.

Ok, it hurts too much to care. "Yep, cracked it right down the middle." I lean back with my hands on my hips to get my balance.

He pinches the bridge of his nose, but at least he chuckles. "Grab a drink of water and go work on headers."

Yes, that's what I need... a soccer ball to the head to knock some sense into me.

* * *

My bumbum is still a little sore Sunday morning. I sit numbly through church... the service nearly over, Pastor Reyes' voice muffles beneath my loud thoughts. The image of my "expected family contribution" is plastered to my brain, front and center. I haven't even told my mom and dad about that. When the congregation says a collective "Amen," I glance at the pulpit, weirded-out by the fact that I hadn't even realized we'd been praying. Xavier and Amber squeeze my hand, then both look at me, heads tilted. I'm usually the hand squeezer in this group.

"Still basking in the glow of your acceptance?" Tyler doesn't stop holding Amber's hand after the post-Amen squeeze. They never let go.

"Yeah, I guess I am." More like shell-shocked by the giant bill the Worry Monster is screaming about repeatedly in my mind.

Mom hunts for the keys in her purse as she turns in her pew to speak to us. "See you kids in a little bit. I made lasagna for lunch and brownies for dessert." She loves when I have friends over. Giddiness lights up her face. She leans toward Xavier and adds, "I picked up some vanilla ice cream and hot fudge to go with your brownie, hun." Oh, mom.

Xavier, Tyler, and Amber make their way to the parking lot while I follow my parents to the car. I miss my art distraction from yesterday.

Thankfully, once we're all stuffed with garlic bread, lasagna, and double chocolate chip brownies, my friends and I file into the living room and arrange all the cushions so we're in a make-shift movie-watching fort, with tons of blankets and extra pillows. Sadly, the James' don't own a tortilla blanket, but then again, at least no one has to fight over it.

Tyler grabs the remote and scrolls through the streaming options. "Commodore's choice today, so what are we watching, Liv? *Mamma Mia, Hunger Games,* a little *Harry Potter* action?"

So many options. "Hmmm... what about something classic like *Mean Girls* or—"

"What about *Shrek?*" Xavier interrupts.

"NO!"

Good grief, did someone just yell that?

Me, I yelled. I clear my throat as I take in their wide eyes, seemingly shocked at my unexpected outburst. Why is my neck impossibly hot?

"Sorry, ogre aversion." That is so far from the truth. "Let's pick another movie, shall we?"

The awkward silence lingers, because since when do I blurt out like that? "What about *Cutting Edge?* It's a perfect wintery day movie with an angsty romance, and my mom swears it's a classic."

"A chick flick?" Tyler groans. But when Amber says, "Awww... sounds great," at nearly the same time, he's quick to change his tone. They're adorable and I struggle to ignore the wave of envy that forms deep in my gut.

While Xavier, Tyler, and Amber spread out amongst my family's ancient sectional sofa fort, I hang out on the floor on a squishy bean bag, a big bowl of popcorn in my lap. The film is near the juicy point, where Kate and Doug are about to declare their love for one another and, spoiler alert, complete a perfect Pamchenko, when Xavier leans down and whispers in my ear. "I wanna see your acceptance letter before I leave. And don't get shy on me either, you know you want to show it off."

Prayers up that he doesn't notice the goosebumps I can feel on the skin of my neck that popped up from his proximity. I take my hair out of my ponytail just in case. It would be easier for ME to pull off a Pamchenko–solo– than pay to attend Vandy, but sure, I'll pretend I'm not devastated and celebrate an empty victory with my bestie. Why not?

As the credits roll, Xavier heads down the hall, straight to my room. I rush to catch up to him and find him in front of my desk, his smile contagious. I step next to him and he puts an arm around me, then gives my shoulder a squeeze. When he drops his hand, I miss it immediately.

Snap out of it, this is Xavier.

"What are these?" He looks at the flyers on my desk and picks one up to study it.

We repeat the same conversation I had with my mom yesterday, minus the whole "Who is Paul" part. The difference in this conversation and the one earlier is Xavier's clenched jaw. It's hard to understand his angst against the Ogre, so I divert.

"Let's go back to the living room with everyone else." I place my hand on his arm so he'll lower the flier, but when he drops it on my desk, it grazes the mousepad on my Chromebook and the monitor buzzes to life, opening to the dreaded "expected financial contributions" page. I slam my Chromebook shut and cross my arms over my chest. Please Lord, I pray Xavier didn't see that outlandish number.

I look up at Xavier and... nothing. I don't know if he saw it or not, but he's staring at me. Like, into my soul. It's unnerving. I swallow. "So... bet you've got a ton of home-work tonight, huh?"

His brows furrow and he shakes his head slightly. "We have half of the same classes and you know I don't have homework."

"Right. It's my other classes that have homework." Gulp. I can hear Amber and Tyler laughing down the hall. I lean over to peek out the door, wishing Xavier would take the hint and head back out with them, then turn to face him again.

"You ok, Liv?" He tucks a loose strand of hair behind my ear. "You seem a little off."

I've got to get it together. "Sorry. I just have a lot on my mind."

"Do you wanna talk about it?"

"No. Yes?" When he raises his eyebrows, I continue. "Can I text you later?"

He stares a beat too long for comfort and I squirm under his scrutiny. "Anytime, Liv. You know that."

I do. But I don't think I can, not about this...

* * *

THIS being that crazy, terrible idea that's been living rent free in my mind since the second I clicked the financial aid information after I got my acceptance letter.

My friends left hours ago. Now, my phone sits to my right, begging me to text or call Xavier so he can walk me off this ledge. To my right, the finished flyers I'd scanned and sent to Nurse Underwood. And right in front of me, my Chromebook, open to the Wonderbrink Foundations Diabetes Scholarship page... an online application, a letter of recommendation from a current teacher, and a 500-word essay requirement. It's almost too easy.

I click back to the screen with the giant number.

Then back to the Wonderbrink site.

Then back to the giant number.

Ugh.

I pick up my phone to text Xavier, horrified by my own actions. My fingers hover over the keypad on my phone, but instead of Xavier, I text Paul.

> Me: Tell me more about your diabetes journey, Ogre.

> Paul: Not sure what your endgame is, Donkey, but that info will cost you a coffee at Beans & Books.

Did we just accidentally agree to a low-key date, or did I just receive an invoice for a diabetes interview?

> Me: Deal.

> Paul: See you tomorrow at 4.

I start to respond, "It's a date," then delete it, because... is it a date?

> Me: 4 it is.

And then, since maybe I'm a horrible person, I print the instructions for the teacher's letter of recommendation and fold it neatly in my binder, tucking it away in my backpack for school tomorrow.

What am I even doing?

Chapter 6
Very Superstitious

"When you believe in things
That you don't understand,
Then you suffer,
Superstition ain't the way..."
-Stevie Wonder, Superstitious

I barely slept last night, thinking about the scholarship and staring at the clock, always a huge mistake when one can't fall asleep. Oddly, I'm not tired. I force myself to focus on notes and labs all morning, then avoid conversation at lunch. It's Motivational Monday in psychology class, and we're tasked with viewing and discussing a TED Talk.

Halfway through the lecture, Xavier sticks a pale yellow post-it note on the corner of my binder. This note has the letter "L" in the center, and the number fifteen in the top corner. My pencil traces mindless doodles all around the letter, fanning out to create a mandala type design. Why does class seem to be taking so long today?

As soon as the dismissal bell rings, I head straight for the teacher's desk. "Mr. Winters?"

He pauses typing whatever he's working on at his computer and gives me his full attention. "Yes, Olivia?"

"Would you be willing to fill out this recommendation to the Wonderbrink Foundation for me? It's for a college scholarship. You just write a general letter and submit it directly on their website or mail it using this self-addressed, stamped envelope." *And please, please, PUH-LEASE don't probe me for more information.*

Mr. Winters pushes his glasses up on the bridge of his nose and studies the paper for a beat. "Sure thing, Miss James. I'm honored you asked and I'll get right on it."

Deep breath.

"Thank you." Now to make haste for the exit—I turn and hightail it out of the room.

Except I run straight into Xavier, who catches me by the shoulders. "Whoa, there." Was he waiting for me?

"Oh my gosh, Xavier, you scared me!" My fingers tighten around my binder, pulling it close to my chest.

"What was that about?" He grabs my phone as it slides off the top of my books, then tucks it under my chin. "You didn't text last night and you've been super quiet all day. Everything okay?"

"Peachy. I'm sorry. I've been working on some scholarship stuff. Vandy is exciting, but it's also expensive." Well, at least that's not a lie, but these secrets, ugh.

"Gotcha. You and Amber coming to the game tonight?"

"Of course. Wouldn't miss it." And I'm going to cheer extra loud to make up for missing the last one.

His satisfied smirk does something funny to my tummy. I will absolutely be at his game, I just have to grab some coffee on my pseudo-date first.

"I can't wait for your game. And... I'm meeting Paul at Beans & Books after school." A flutter of guilt passes through my midsection, and I press my books into my stomach to make it stop.

Xavier pauses a beat, then gives a small nod. "Have fun."

When the tardy bell rings to remind us we're supposed to be on opposite sides of the school in two minutes, I readjust my arm full of supplies and offer him a half-hearted smile before I turn to walk away.

"Olivia, wait!" Xavier blurts and I turn back to him. He starts to say something, then closes his mouth. Softly, he adds, "Drive safe, okay?"

"Of course, always." What was that about? And if my stomach doesn't stop fluttering, there's no way I'm drinking coffee after school.

* * *

I adjust my knitted scarf as I open the door to Beans & Books and search the seats for Paul. He's waiting on a giant leather sofa across from the walls of books, engrossed in his phone. Punctuality is a point in his favor. A flutter of nerves makes my mouth go dry, but I tamp down the feeling. This is *not* a date. We're two friends hanging out, discussing a disease he doesn't realize I most certainly do not have. That's all.

"Hi Paul."

"Donkey." He gives me the universal boy code for "hey," a barely discernible head nod.

"Should we order? What's on the menu in this swamp? Weed rats, flies, slugs..."

"Donkey has jokes, I see. You're hilarious." He deadpans, barely cracking a grin.

Before he can say anything else, his phone beeps. He takes a peek, then scowls and taps on the device. He clicks a few buttons in an app and shakes his head. "Sorry. This stupid CGM still isn't working right. Can we wait to order so I can check my blood sugar?"

"Of course." I lay my coat and other outerwear over the arm of the chair next to him, then take my seat. I fiddle with the leaf of a potted plant on the small table beside me while Paul opens a black case and takes out a small device. He pricks his finger, applies a drop of blood to a test strip, and waits for the meter to give a reading. I look away to hide my concern, but that has to hurt. Right? Why can't someone fix the monitor thingy he used at the basketball game?

After he finishes, we walk to the counter, and Paul stays in front of me. Thank goodness my new friend isn't exactly chivalrous, because I really don't want to order first.

"My usual."

The barista nods. "One tall caffè macchiato with

sugar free vanilla syrup and two Splenda, coming right up."

Paul grabs a spoon, pays for himself, and then moves to the side so I can order. Ok, so, definitely not a date.

The barista, no nonsense and somewhat indifferent when she took Paul's order, offers me a warm smile.

"Hi. I'd like a Phish food hot cocoa, please." Oh! "With sugar free chocolate syrup." Am I doing this right? Paul gives me an odd look, but maybe it's because I didn't order coffee. My stomach is already in knots, so no thank you.

We return to the sofa and I watch as he uses his spoon to scoop at some invisible ingredient on the surface of his drink.

Not once.

Not twice.

But thrice.

"Um, what are you doing?" I look around to see if anyone else has noticed his odd behavior. Seriously, what is happening right now?

"Donkey, everyone knows that catching bubbles in your coffee with a spoon and eating them brings good luck."

"Everyone absolutely does not, because I've never heard of that in my life. And Ogre, I don't believe in luck."

He clutches his chest like I've wounded him, eyes wide. "How can you not?"

"And undermine my hard work?"

He shuts his mouth. "Your loss." Then shrugs and swallows a fourth spoonful of caffeinated air pockets.

I shake my head. "Moving on. I know it was probably weird that I'm asking, but can you tell me about your experience with diabetes?"

Paul's eyes narrow—he's practically squinting—and his mouth crimps shut in one corner. Did I go too far? Is he suspicious?

"I wasn't born with diabetes, remember?" Or diagnosed with it, but at least I'm not telling a lie.

"Right. Uh, sure. Having diabetes is like living in a never-ending game of 'Guess How Much Insulin I Need' while simultaneously dodging everyone's unsolicited advice."

I bite back a frown—his response is not what I was expecting. "That's got to be irritating. What's the weirdest advice you've ever gotten?"

"Oh, it's definitely annoying. 'Have you tried not having diabetes?' is a real gem I've received. Like, Oh, why didn't I think of that? As if I can help it that my pancreas doesn't pull its weight."

"I can't believe someone would say something *that* ignorant. What helps?"

"Sarcasm."

He would say that. "Sarcasm can be endearing."

"Thanks, Donkey, I'll add that to my list of reasons to keep it around. Let's just say I became very well acquainted with my insulin pump. My permanent sidekick is obsessed with making sure I never forget to eat or check my blood sugar. At least it is when it manages to work correctly."

"Have you ever considered naming your pump?"

It's hard to miss the mischievous little twinkle in his

eye when he deadpans, "Her name's Fiona and I love her."

I snort, because that's a perfect name for Paul's pump. "Biggest challenge?"

"Probably trying to explain to people that my need for snacks at odd hours isn't just me being moody. I've become an expert at balancing what I eat and when. And I hate when the guys ask if they can eat my snacks."

"*That* sounds annoying. Any advice for someone just learning about diabetes?"

Paul places his mug on the table between us, crosses his arms, and looks at me funny. Is seventeen too late for a diabetes diagnosis? Maybe I should have done more research.

"Well, if you ask my stepmom, she'd feed you some garbage like, 'Remember that diabetes is a part of you are, but it doesn't define you.' But really, preparation is my best advice. Always, always have snacks. You never know when your blood sugar might go loco."

"Snacks are life, Paul." I don't think he realizes how serious I am when I say this. He just doesn't know my love of snacks has nothing to do with diabetes. "And thank you for helping me out."

"No problem." Paul chuckles. "Welcome to your new normal."

If he only knew. "So, what are your plans for next year?"

"No idea." My mouth parts and I quickly shut it. How is he so nonchalant about his lack of future plans?

Really? No clue? And if this were a date, wouldn't he ask me something about me and my interests?

He picks up his mug. "What's the plan for Commodore Donkey?" There it is. So maybe this little get-together is date-ish?

"I'm going to study illustrative art in Nashville, following in the footsteps of one of Vanderbilt's famous alumni, Paige O'Donnell."

Paul chokes on his drink and I grab a handful of napkins. "You ok?"

"Oh, I'm just dandy." He coughs but recovers quickly.

I grab napkins from the table dispenser and help wipe up the brown liquid off the tabletop while I continue. "I discovered her art when I was a little girl and I've loved it ever since. Creating art is my happy place, ya know?"

He raises a brow. "I do not know, but I get the impression you do. I'm related to someone with illustrative art talent."

"Yeah?"

"Yeah. I'll have to introduce you—."

"Heeeeyyyyyy, Paul." A beautiful girl about our age in a CHS letter jacket walks past, waving her dainty, perfectly manicured fingers, then winks. Her high-gloss entourage bursts into feminine giggles. Paul offers his signature nod, complete with a smirk, and watches as they walk away. So, not a date. Not even close. This is the whole *belly buttons at the basketball game* situation he was so bemused by all over again. Dudes don't flirt when they're with someone else.

After that metaphorical record scratch, I retrieve my scarf and sling it around my neck.

Awkward silence for a beat, then I sneak a glance at the time on my phone. "Sorry to run, but I need to pick up Amber so we can get to Xavier and Tyler's basketball game."

Something flickers in his expression and I swear his grip tightens around his empty cup. "We should hang out again sometime."

I freeze as I pull my hat over my head. My cheeks flush and my posture is suddenly stiff as my fuzzy thoughts reconsider all that has happened over the last half hour. Now he's asking me out? Was this a date and I didn't know it? 'Cause it sure felt more like an interview for a school newspaper than anything remotely romantic.

Oh, why not? "Solid plan, Ogre."

* * *

"Let's go cheer for our men." Amber's statement causes me to nearly inhale my gum as she climbs into my passenger seat and pulls out a plain shirt and a sharpie marker from a plastic shopping bag. The theme for tonight's game is "Little White Lies." I take in her shirt, which reads, "I'm not emotionally invested in this game."

Right, like she won't be one of the loudest fans in the gym. Along with me, of course. "What should I write on my shirt?"

"Hmmm... how about 'Vandy is for losers' or 'I'm not in love with my best friend?'"

"Amber!" I hiss, nearly swerving the car into oncoming traffic.

"What?" Her innocent tone is anything but.

"Please don't say crazy stuff like that."

She cocks her head. "Don't tell me you haven't noticed Xavier's been acting differently since you started hanging out with Paul. I'm not a fan, by the way."

I blink. "What? Why? You hardly know the guy." Heck, I hardly know the guy.

"First of all, he isn't Xavier, and I'm still waiting for you two to come to your senses and declare your love for one another."

The heat of a deep blush covers me from my head to the tips of my toes. "Seriously, where is this suddenly coming from? You know I don't feel that way anymore." I absolutely do, but I have buried those feelings deeper than the bottom of the Mariana trench. At least I thought they were, but Amber can read me like a book, it seems.

Amber counts off on her fingers. "And secondly, anyone that superstitious has got to have some serious anxiety issues."

"Lots of people have anxiety issues. That's not a character flaw."

"And they deal with their anxiety in healthier ways. I mean, all that superstitious mumbo-jumbo junk is pure ignorance. Third, he's a little too self-absorbed." She crosses her arms and studies me.

I work my jaw back and forth, keeping my focus on the road. "I wish you'd tell me how you really feel, Amber."

"I *feel* like you should pray for Paul to grow in wisdom, then distance yourself from him and tell Xavier you like him as more than a friend."

My fingers tighten around the steering wheel. "Is that all?"

She turns in her seat to face me. "So, you're not denying your feelings? That's a big step, Liv. Huge. I'm proud of you."

I growl as I pull into the high school parking lot and put the car in park. My head drops against the steering wheel as delicate snowflakes begin to dot the windshield. "How about 'Entitled rich kid?' Can I put that on my shirt?"

"Just because someone has money doesn't necessarily mean they're entitled."

I turn my head, still resting on the wheel. "Oh my gosh, Amber. I was kidding. How about 'My best friend never gets on my nerves?'"

"The point is to write a little white lie, sweetie." She blinks at me, guilelessness evident in her eyes, then grins.

I uncap the permanent marker and pen "Art is over-rated" on my shirt, throw it on over top of my hoodie, and then we head into the game.

* * *

"My boyfriend is so clutch," Amber declares to the nearly empty parking lot. The game was a blowout and many fans left early. The delicate flakes from earlier made quick work of morphing into an unexpected snow blanket.

Tyler smiles smugly as he scans a weather app on his phone. "If this keeps up, there's no way we're having school tomorrow."

Amber whispers loudly, "I bet Paul already has his pajamas on inside out and he's flushing ice-cubes down the potty as we speak."

I try my best not to react, but Xavier snorts, so I shoot him the stink eye.

Amber turns her focus back to me. "Wanna sleep over, Liv? I have extra toothbrushes and if they don't cancel, you can always borrow some of my clothes?"

Right, because I'm not over half a foot taller than my petite pal.

"Xavier, we should, like, totally have a sleepover, too!" Tyler adds. "We can paint each other's nails pink, share our deepest darkest secrets, and eat Nutella from the jar." He blinks his eyes rapidly and tilts his head to the side.

"Oh em gee, can we put those little nose strip things on too?" Xavier claps his hands together and kicks up a heel, toe inward in a feminine stance. He looks ridiculous posing that way, especially while wearing his basketball warmups.

Amber puts a palm out. "Stop. We all know you're going to smell each other's farts, play hours of video games, and see who can out snore the other while you stare at the back of your eyelids." Having twin older brothers, I can verify these are all highly likely.

"Gross." Xavier wrinkles his nose. Tyler rolls his eyes before he leans over to kiss Amber on the temple, then he starts his truck. In this weather, it's going to need time to warm up.

Xavier pulls me into an unexpected hug. "Thanks for coming," he says, then hops in with Tyler.

We watch the boys drive away, the heat from the truck's exhaust making giant puffs of smoke in the snowy sky. "Don't start," I say to Amber when she glances at me with her told-you-so expression. "And yes to a girl's night. I just need to text my parents."

"Atta girl." She grins as she climbs into my car.

We stay up entirely too late considering there's no guarantee they'll cancel school tomorrow. I borrow some PJs and we settle in for a movie–*Legally Blonde*–but barely watch, focusing instead on important girl talk.

Amber is sitting on her living room floor, one knee bent and the other leg out while she paints her toes a lovely shade of metallic lavender. "You never told me about your date with Paul."

I hug a pillow to my chest. "That's because I'm not sure it was a date. But I'm pretty sure he asked me out before I left."

"You're *pretty sure?* How do you not know?"

I fill her in on his gorgeous classmates who walked by and his lack of flirty behavior toward me, but share nothing about our diabetes talk. I also leave out that our conversation was pretty one-sided, seeing as how she's already not a huge Paul fan.

"Hmmm... that is weird." She bites her bottom lip. "What would you say if Xavier asked you out?"

Yes, in a heartbeat.

"Amber, Xavier hasn't asked me out. He's never acted like he wants to." I sigh.

"But what if–"

"Please, Amber. I didn't sign up for this conversation." Or this trembling chin, but here we are.

Amber screws the lid to her polish back onto the bottle, then sets it on the coffee table. "But you're in it now, and it's only me. I have a yucky feeling about Paul and I know you think I'm crazy, but you and Xavier have been best friends for so long..."

"I'd like to keep it that way."

She lifts an eyebrow. "Really? Even if you could be best friends *and* a couple? How do you know he doesn't feel the same way? What if you're both scared and missing out on something amazing? We're way past freshman year."

"You don't think I haven't thought of that?" Oh good grief, eyes, get it together. I don't want to tear up over this. "What if I miss out on something with Paul because I refuse to accept that Xavier doesn't like me like that?"

"So, you do like Paul?" The skepticism in her voice matches the look on her face.

I pick up the pillow, shove my face in the soft fabric, and let out a long groan.

Once I pull the cushion down from my face, Amber reaches over and gives my hand a squeeze. Then she passes me the jar of Nutella as we turn our attention back to Elle Woods and her message of female empowerment. We know how valuable Elle Woods can be.

* * *

It's a good thing Tyler doesn't have aspirations in meteorology, because school was not, in fact, canceled. Although we did get to sleep in thanks to a two-hour delay. Why do we even have school on days like this? It took twice as long as normal to get from Amber's house to the parking lot. I'm wearing one of her oversized dance shirts and a pair of skinny jeans that are not nearly as comfortable as my usual soccer pants. Xavier looks at me funny when he notices my outfit in fourth-period psychology.

"You look, like, totally adorbs!" Tyler places his hand out his jutted-out hip, his voice high. Amber scoffs at his impersonation, clearly offended, and he scratches the back of his neck.

I press my lips together and resist the urge to roll my eyes. This feels eerily similar to that time I participated in a ballet workshop Amber's dance studio hosted as a fundraiser before a big showcase. All I remember from that experience are French words, unnatural poses, and pain. It reinforced both my respect for Amber's talent and my love of soccer.

Thankfully, Mr. Winters saves Tyler from further conversation. "Class, seeing as how we're on a modified schedule, we don't have time for a complete lesson. Let's call this a Talk-it-Out Tuesday. Please take out a blank sheet of paper and use the next three minutes to jot down a psychology topic you'd like to discuss further. Or you may also write a question you'd like me to try to answer. I'll start the clock now."

He walks around the room as we ponder his assignment. When he announces, "You cannot ask 'Why are we at school today?'" about a third of the class crumples up their work or scribbles it out. When he stops at my desk, he nods, picks up my paper, and heads to the front.

"Ladies and gentlemen, let's start with this topic." He

pulls the cap off of a dry erase marker and writes, "Superstitions." Several of my classmates lift their heads, seemingly intrigued. "Why might an otherwise logical, educated person subscribe to superstitions? What are some common superstitions you guys have heard of?"

Jimmy raises his hand. "If you break a mirror, you get seven years of bad luck."

"Well, then don't look in one," someone in the back jokes.

"Not cool." Mr. Winters gives the offender a stern look. "Good one about the mirror, Jimmy. What else?"

"Don't cross the path of a black cat. Don't walk under a ladder." Amber's on a roll.

"Good, good." He writes their examples on the board. "But why do people believe those? Why would someone knock on wood or throw salt over their shoulder?"

Logan Pitmann, the giant left tackle on the BHS football team, chimes in from the table behind mine. "'Cause people be believin' in luck and weird shi–"

"I'm going to stop you right there, Logan. Please watch your mouth. Solid definition, but in the world of psychology, superstitions are about *control*. People who subscribe to superstitious beliefs tend to do so because they want more certainty in their lives. They demonstrate a tendency to look for a standard or a reason as to why things happen, or don't have... an explanation, if you will. They're glorified coping mechanisms people use to deal with uncertainty or unpredictability."

I lean back in my chair and tap the eraser end of my pencil against my desktop. Is that why Paul's so superstitious? He doesn't have stability in his life? Maybe it's about his parents or diabetes. Or is there something else?

"Y'all, believe it or not, but we're all susceptible to superstitions." Mr. Winters continues, "Think of famous athletes. Serena Williams, the world-renowned tennis player, always ties her shoes a specific way and bounces the ball exactly five times before she serves. Michael Jordan was known to always wear his college shorts under his Chicago Bulls uniform.

"It's ironic that superstitions are often born out of a lack of control, but usually end up causing more stress and anxiety."

Logan raises his gigantic, muscular arm again. "You mean I ain't got to wear my lucky drawers to my football games no 'mo?"

"Please don't. In fact, burn those." I and several of my classmates giggle at his candor. "You work hard at practice, right?"

"I sho' as shi–" Logan clears his throat before he nearly makes the same mistake twice. "Yes, sir, real hard."

"Then why not take credit for your strong work ethic instead of a false belief that a pair of old thread-bare Hanes can run a route like you?"

Logan grins at that. "Ayyyyeeee, yes sir."

Before Mr. Winters can entertain other topics or questions, the bell rings.

Fourth period might be over, but my concern about Paul's superstitions is far from it.

Chapter 7
Happy Palentine's Day, Sir

The snow having mostly melted, the Core Four pile into a booth at the back of the Reyes Panaderya Thursday evening after practice. There is a massive spread of all of our favorite appetizers in the center of our table. Single status or not, I've always, *always*, loved Valentine's Day. (To be fair, I love all holidays. I'm an equal opportunity holiday celebrate-er). So maybe the real St. Valentine was no patron of love, but I like the modern-day interpretation. Chocolate, flowers, cards, give me all the things.

Starting around sixth-grade, Amber and I began celebrating *Galentine's* Day, and later, around eighth grade, we absorbed Xavier and a then strictly platonic Tyler and the celebration morphed into *Palentine's* Day. Even Pippa gets pink heart-shaped dog-treats for *Pawlentine's* Day. She eats that stuff up too, literally and figuratively.

Even though Amber and Tyler now celebrate a more traditional Valentine's Day, we still exchange gifts as the

Core Four. This year, I bought Tyler and Amber a gift certificate to Flow & Glow, a date night experience where couples can design their own candle, mix the scent, blend it with the wax, name it, the whole shebang. It's perfect because Amber is a total mush-fest like me and Tyler is a low-key pyro. I hand painted their card. Obviously. The front has Tyler in his football gear twirling Amber in a dance leotard.

Amber opens their gift and clasps her hands at her chest. "Oh my gosh, thank you!" She delights in running her fingers over the embellished font of the fancy certificate. Tyler is smiling too, but his grin seems a wee bit more maniacal than joyful. Maybe a flammable present wasn't the best idea for someone who gets a little too happy about Fourth of July fireworks every summer. Meh, they both seem pretty thrilled, so my job here is done.

"Open yours," Amber insists, pushing a small, rose-colored box my way.

I rip away the pink wrapping paper and find they've combined their gift to me—a leather-bound sketchbook with pink hearts embossed on the front and a posable drawing figure. "You guys are the best, thank you!" I resist the overwhelming urge to embrace everyone in a giant group hug, afraid I'd make the happy couple uncomfortable. Or at least the Tyler half.

Tyler spears a pork siomai from a platter and points his fork in my direction. "Now you can stop pining away for the mannequin in the lounge at work when you doodle during breaks."

Xavier chokes on a wing because, honestly, out of

context, that probably sounded a little weird. But he's not wrong.

Next, Amber and Tyler give Xavier a Valentine-themed gift card to Craving the Curls, his favorite—and *the world's best*, his words—ice cream shop, and according to him, one hundred percent worth the drive to Paducah to enjoy. Which is funny, because I also bought him a gift certificate to Craving the Curls. For his card, I drew a comic of him eating a giant cone of Soft-Serve with the words "To my legen-dairy best friend" in melty bubble letters. You can't go wrong gifting Xavier ice cream. He must agree, based on how quickly he shoves the cards into his wallet, grinning like a Cheshire cat.

Xavier's gift to Tyler and Amber are custom made socks with each other's faces on them. I suspect his sister helped with those, but his gifts also knocked it out of the park. It's a safe bet Tyler will wear them to school tomorrow with slides. The cringe...

I bask in the knowledge that everyone seems to like their gifts. It's a huge relief too—they took a significant chunk of my most recent Grace & Glimmer paycheck.

"Last but not least." Xavier slides a thick red envelope my direction, my name scribbled in his boyish hand-writing on the front. I gently break the seal and open the card, setting aside two shiny Comic-Con tickets, and read his poem aloud:

> *Roses are red,*
> *Violets are blue,*
> *Comic-Con is back,*
> *And poetry is hard...so I bought these*

tickets for you because we went when we were little and you loved it.

Tyler grabs my card and reads Xavier's words aloud. "When you become the poet laureate one day, I'm going to tell people I knew you when..." Tyler has his mouth full, again, burning the end of his BBQ pork skewer in the flame of the table's tea light candle. Amber, elusive to her boyfriend's exploits, is staring at the two of us, hearts pouring out of her eyes. I ignore her.

Batting my lashes at Xavier, I ask, "Are you going to wear tight leggings like your dad and Uncle Angelo did the last time we went to Lexington Comic-Con?"

"You wish, but sadly, no." He smirks. "And good news. You don't have to drive all the way to Lexington because Comic-con is in Paducah this year."

I grab the tickets to read the fine details and sure enough, Comic-Con is two weeks away in none other than Paducah, Kentucky. Less than one measly little hour away.

"Hey." Xavier knocks his knee against mine under the table. I look over and he's got a gleam in his eye. "Paige O'Donnel has a spotlight session this year. And a featured table."

My mouth opens and closes, twice, but words escape me. I bite down a grin that threatens to take over my face as my insides vibrate. No force of nature could stop me from an inevitable display of affection. I wrap my arms around him in a giant hug. When he wraps his arms around me, I feel his chest shaking with laughter.

"Gross, get a room." Amber is eyeing us and Tyler is smirking.

We break apart and I stare at the tickets until the words go fuzzy and my mouth hurts from grinning.

Xavier clears his throat and I glance at his pained expression. "They're your tickets, Liv. I don't want you to think you can't take whoever you want."

"Xavier! Are you trying to get out of Comic-Con?" My eyes grow wide and I turn in my seat to face him full on. "You're my best friend, you have to go."

His features relax and a smile takes over his handsome face again. "I didn't want to assume anything."

Is he talking about Paul? Did he really think I'd want to take someone else?

"We can stop by Craving the Curl on the way home, too." Now his eyes are lit up like a Christmas tree. There's my bestie.

Gah, I absolutely cannot wait for Comic-Con.

Saturday morning, it takes fifteen minutes longer to get to the Sugar Shatterers meeting because it's like twenty degrees outside and I'm terrified of black ice. When the twins were seniors, they were sideswiped by some guy in a pick-up truck who left a giant dent in the side of their truck, then drove off. Left my brothers stranded in a ditch, and left an even bigger dent in my parent's bank account. I'd rather not re-live the anxiety of that whole crazy experience, so I drive like a hypervigilant grandma all the way to Cadiz.

It's freezing when I get out of the car at Bluegrass Baptist, so I carefully do a quick but cautious shuffle in my winter boots all the way to the door, gasping on the frigid air as I go. Thank you, employee discount, for footwear fit for snow. I've become a master at the revolving door, too, and I appreciate the blast of scorching heat it offers when I make it through.

Despite the human blow-dryer experience, I'm still shivering when I take my seat in the meeting room. All eyes are on me as my entrance interrupts Nurse Underwood.

"Um, I'm sorry. I hope I didn't miss anything." I take my seat and Paul passes a tray with sugar free, diabetic friendly muffins. "Oh my gosh," I whisper, "Are you... the muffin man?"

"The muffin man?" He raises his eyebrows.

"The muffin man."

He blinks. "Oh good grief, Donkey, make it stop." But then he hums the "*...lives on Drury Lane,*" portion of the song, so I get the impression he's not all that annoyed. And the muffin man looks quite fetching in his gray cable-knit sweater. Dudes in sweaters are way under-rated, in my humble opinion.

"...Olivia made these awesome flyers for our fundrais-er." I peel my eyes off Paul and feel my cheeks heat at the attention. Nurse Underwood has the flyers I designed pulled up on the screen.

Paul's mouth hangs open as he looks at the television. "Dang, Donkey, you weren't kidding. You really are talented in illustrative art."

The sincerity in his voice takes me by surprise, and my ears burn from his praise. It's hard to focus on the rest of the meeting. And it's a good thing the meeting isn't terribly long, because when I reach into my bag for my keys, they're not there. I dig in my bag, my coat pockets, then scan under the seat of my chair.

Paul tilts his head in my direction, brows furrowed. "What? What's wrong?"

"I can't find my keys."

"Did you lock them in your car?"

"No. Well, I mean... I don't think so." My cheeks are scorching.

When we exit the building and walk toward my car, we approach the driver's side door, and my stomach falls. There is my cute little Vandy keychain dangling in the ignition. I must have left it running. Clearly, the battery is dead.

I run my hands down my red-hot face and let out a groan. "Do you have any jumper cables?"

Paul mutters something under his breath and his jaw tenses up. "I don't, but I can call my dad."

"Thank you."

Paul pulls out a shiny, ridiculously fancy phone and makes the call. I pick up only bits and pieces, but he's standing rod straight and his micro-movements seem a little stiff. "Yes sir...an acquaintance from the diabetes support group... no sir... yes sir... we're right outside." He hangs up and starts pacing. That was a whole lot of "sirs."

Not two minutes later a serious looking man in an expensive, tailor-made suit marches up to us. His identification badge reads *Doctor Geoffrey Roberts, President of Bluegrass Baptist Health Hospital.*

Whoa. Paul's dad is the president of Bluegrass Baptist Health? Bougie.

"Paul." He nods stiffly, then turns to me and extends a hand. "And you must be Miss …?"

"James." I shake his hand with what I hope is more firm than sweaty, then promptly reach for my gloves. "Er, Miss James. Of course my actual name isn't James." Oh my gosh, why can't I make my mouth stop? And why did I refer to myself as "miss?"

"Sir, Miss James is an acquaintance from Sugar Shatterers." Such formality. Paul's standing like he's a soldier at bootcamp about to be inspected by his commanding officer.

Dr. Roberts removes a key fob from his pocket and the lights from an impeccably clean Mercedes two rows over beeps to life from its designated spot. I watch in mortified fascination as Paul and his dad work to jump my humble little Honda. When she's finally resurrected, his dad instructs him to follow me home and tells me not to turn the radio on.

Silence is cool. There are already sirens going off in my head, so I'm not sure I'd hear any music, anyway.

Over half a quiet hour later–again, black ice–I pull into my driveway. Paul parks his way-too-nice-for-any-teenager SUV behind me and walks around to my door.

Can I roll my window down? Will that somehow mess up my jumped battery? I open the door instead but leave the car running. I swing my legs around and rest my feet on the running board so I can face Paul.

He rests an arm on the roof of my car. "This your swamp, Donkey?"

"No, I just liked the sign."

"Funny. You can turn your car off now, but make sure your dad or somebody checks your battery."

I make a great show of taking the keys from the ignition and offer him my best side-eye. "Ogre, it's almost like you care."

He snorts. "Of course, I care." I wonder if he can see Xavier's Palentine's day envelope in my passenger seat. If he does, what does he think? Does it matter if he cares or not?

"So, your dad is the President of the hospital."

With a roll of his eyes, Paul nods. "Yes ma'am."

I smile at his mock manners. "I guess your dad can be a little intense."

"A little? Extreme hard-core would be more accurate."

That scares me enough to ask, "Paul, your dad's never, like... hurt—"

His shoulders fall, but he shakes his head, a sad smile on his handsome face. "No. Nothing like that. My dad wouldn't hurt a fly. The crushing weight of his expectations, though, that might destroy a guy."

"I'm sorry." I hate that for him. It's not that my parents don't have high expectations, but they took me to get a milkshake when I passed my driver's test after my second attempt. To them, even failure can be fruitful.

Mom chooses that moment to let Pippa out the front door to do her business. Excited about a new human to slobber on, she wastes no time running around to the side of my car to investigate. Odd that she stops abruptly when she sees Paul. Instead of sniffing and licking him into oblivion, she holds back, sitting on her haunches. She doesn't growl, but her uptight posture screams skepticism.

Paul doesn't seem too excited to see her either. In fact, he mostly ignores her while my mom catches up to her and attaches the leash to her collar. He looks Pippa over from head to tail, then he shakes his head. "You would own a four-legged free-loader."

Oh-no-he-didn't. He did not call my baby a four-legged freeloader! I don't even know how to respond. Pippa, however, barks once then pulls Mom off toward their usual walking route.

Mom and I stare, wide-eyed, at the brief exchange. I'm so shocked by his reference to my furry friend that I forget to introduce him to my mother.

"Well, that's my cue." Paul gives a two-finger salute and heads back to his car.

That's my cue? What? Where's the rigid, well-mannered young man from earlier? When you meet a mom, you shake hands and offer at least two "ma'am"s somewhere in your introduction. And before she came outside, I'd half expected him to declare that dogs are good luck and Pippa's wet nose could cure diabetes and bring world peace, but that would be ridiculous. Before he closes the door to his car, I shake out of my stupor and shout, "Someday I will repay you. Unless, of course, I can't find you, or if I forget."

He pauses as he climbs into his car and offers a lazy grin in approval. "Nice *Shrek* 2 reference, Donkey."

"I try." And I don't know if I *can* repay him, so his nonchalance is somewhat of a relief. I walk over to stand beside mom, still processing that odd encounter.

"What was that about? Was that Paul? Why did he follow you home?" Pippa is losing her mind waiting for her walk.

"My car died. Yes. My car died." This is a weird conversation.

"Oh no, that's not good. Let's check your battery after I walk Pippa." She surrenders to Pippa's relentless pulling and sets off down the street.

My phone buzzes in my coat pocket as I step inside my quaint but blissfully warm home. It's Xavier.

> Xavier: Hey. You got any away games this week? Just checking to see if you can make it to our game Friday.

> Me: I have a tournament in Elizabethtown all day tomorrow, but nothing except practice the rest of the week.

> Xavier: Good, 'cause we play Cadiz and I need my bestie.

Oh boy.

Chapter 8
Win Some, Lose Some

Oh gosh. My room, normally tidy, has succumbed to chaos—a flurry of motion and noise while I try my best to get ready for this tournament. Two different jerseys rest over the back of my desk chair, a pair of cleats lie on the floor by my bed, and there's a mess of socks and shin guards strewn across my carpet.

"Mom, have you seen my black shorts?" Why do I have four pairs of not-black shorts but I can't find the one pair I need?

"Check the dryer." Mom's voice echoes faintly from down the hall.

Sigh. I run-walk to the laundry room and rummage through the dryer until I find the elusive shorts, still warm from the cycle. (That's the best...) I fold those as I return to my train-wreck of a room and then do one last mental checklist: jerseys, shorts, socks, shin guards, cleats, water bottle, deodorant, snacks.

Sweet.

Last but never least, hair. In the bathroom, I brush and detangle my red heap of curly tresses until they're halfway tame, then grab a handful of clear bands, weaving them around auburn locks until a cute bubble braid is set. Clark once called this style "Ginga Ninja," thinking I'd hate it. I love it. Makes me feel powerful, and it's my go-to tournament arrangement since he christened me with the title.

My phone buzzes quietly on the counter, then buzzes again.

> Xavier: Have fun and be safe. I'll be silently cheering for you from the pews this morning–Go, Liv!

Awww...

> Paul: Good luck today, Donkey. Hope your batteries are better charged than your car.

Uhhh... Is that supposed to be nice, or not? Flirty? Funny? I'm not one of those weird chicks who thinks it's cute when a boy is rude. I don't have time to dissect his words, so I type back a quick "thank you" to both and shove my phone in my duffle bag, then zip it shut.

"Liv, let's go or we're going to be late."

"Coming!" She doesn't have to tell me twice.

In the garage, dad loads my bag into the trunk and hands me a breakfast bar and a bottle of water.

As much as I enjoy soccer, I hate to miss Pastor Reyes' sermon. Don't get me started on the guilt over making Mom and Dad miss church to drive all the way to

Elizabethtown to cheer me on. Not that they'd allow me to drive that far by myself, or that early or late. Plus, I'm a little nervous about driving my own car after I let the battery die yesterday.

Another concern: What if my besties watch a classic film without me this afternoon, like *Teen Wolf* or *10 Things I Hate About You*? Or *Princess Bride*?

Inconceivable. Not only are those first world problems, but my friends would *never* watch such cinematic masterpieces without me. And I can always ask Xavier to give me a summary of his dad's preaching tomorrow at school. Maybe they'll watch an NFL game.

Once we pull into the rec center, I join my team while my parents walk to the bleachers. Right in the middle of our dynamic stretches, someone yells, "Gooooo, Olivia!"

Wait, I know that voice. I scan the crowd and find Matt, Clark, and a beautiful brunette with my parents. They're waving their arms wildly, huge smiles on their faces.

Meagan bumps my shoulder. "Not your usual fan club, huh?"

"Nope, not today. They're all at church." I look back at the twins and Matt is holding the brunette's hand. Awwww. "But my brothers came."

"And Matt brought a girl." She wiggles her eyebrows at me and I grin back. "What about Paul?"

My words flounder for a minute and it's a real effort not to flinch. I purse my lips as I consider my answer. "No Paul." That doesn't stop me from chewing the inside of my cheek and looking over the crowd, but of course he isn't there. Meagan merely nods. Our conversation ends when Coach Lonnie yells his final instructions and sends us out to take our positions on the field. Our team wins the coin toss, granting us first touch. The ref blows his whistle and Meagan and I run. Her ebony ponytail bounces as she dribbles, quick and agile. The opposing teams' defense closes in, their gazes glued to the ball. She kicks it to another midfielder and the action increases. The bright blue of our jerseys blurs as we try our best to keep up. My brothers came, and we're not losing this game. Not on my watch. Actually, that's a heck of a lot of bravado for someone who probably won't play more than half the game, but I'll do what I can.

When there are about ten minutes of time left, Coach Lonnie subs me out again and I take my usual spot on the sidelines. I spray water in my mouth and catch my breath while I cheer for my teammates. The score is still 0-0, but the way my brothers are screaming you'd think it was the world cup. I can't decide if they're yelling crazy stuff because Matt wants to impress the girl he brought or because Clark wants to embarrass our brother in front of her.

"Let's go, Storm! Kick that ball like it owes you money." Oh please. Matt knows I'd jump back in and punt that thing into next week if I thought I could get some spare change for Vandy.

Back on the field, Meagan takes an opportunity to advance and passes the ball, then another teammate dribbles down the sideline to outrun a defender.

"Yes, ladies! You're faster than the rumor mill on a

Monday morning." Where did Clark even come up with that?

I stifle a laugh as our striker, Mia, makes a run toward the goal. She positions herself to meet the ball, then leaps slightly and connects with it at the side of her foot, aiming for the far post. I hold my breath while their goalkeeper dives, but the ball slips just out of her reach and into the back of the net as time expires.

Mia runs the length of the field, then straight into our team huddle—because strikers are the superstars of soccer. An ugly green monster starts to rear its nasty, jealous head, and my ribs squeeze tight.

Refuse to be catty. Refuse to be catty. Refuse *to be catty.*

But as I look over at my family, my brothers are screaming "Let's gooo..." at the top of their lungs, and my negative feelings dissipate. I jog over, join my teammates, and congratulate Mia.

Our win means we play again after lunch. Since we've got awhile, our team walks to the local sandwich shop across the parking lot. You just know they love/hate when a team of hungry athletes shows up. The best part? My family gets to eat with us. The aroma of fresh baked bread hugs me when we walk in. I take a deep breath to appreciate the inviting scents of grilled meats and savory sauces. Soccer can really give a girl an appetite.

I give my brothers hugs as we meet up in the line and search the massive chalk-board menu displayed behind the counter for something to order.

"Liv, I'd like to introduce you to Clara. Clara, this is

Olivia." Matt's cheeks turn an adorable shade of pink and my own cheeks hurt from smiling. I'm so happy for him.

"Nice to meet you, Clara." I hope she doesn't hate the sweaty stench of victory, because my teammates and I are ripe. I put a few extra inches of space between us just in case.

"You too. Great game. I also play midfielder." Clara offers a genuine smile and her easy-going manner meshes seamlessly with Matt's mellow, happy-go-lucky personality. No wonder he seems to like her so much. And if she's good enough for Matt, she's good enough for me.

"No way." I notice her WKU soccer keychain. "You play at Western? You must be really good." And she must really like Matt to go to his little sister's club match if she's talented enough for Division 1. This morning's game being the exception, it's no secret I play left bench more than I play midfielder.

"I do. I met Matt at a Fellowship of Christian Athletes meeting about a month or so ago." Her face practically glows. "He talks about you all the time."

"That's scary." I grin, then place my order. We grab our trays and walk while we talk, then claim seats at a large wooden table with a couple of other soccer families.

"Did you always know you wanted to go to Western?"

Clark rolls his eyes, "Here we go..." I *lightly* kick his shin beneath the table, but based on his dramatic reaction, you'd think I was sawing his right leg off with a rusty spoon.

Clara earns a bonus point for ignoring him as she leans forward with genuine interest. "To be honest, no. I mean, obviously my education is important to me, but so is soccer. I knew I really wanted to play D1. My choices came down to Western or Murray State, and Western offered me the best scholarship package. It was kind of a no-brainer."

I nod. "My best friend Xavier is going to Murray."

"Kind of surprised you're not interested in going to the same place." Someone recovered from his fatal leg injury quickly. Clark's words cause a sudden coldness to hit me in the core, then spread. Why do I feel so exposed? Everyone in my family loves Xavier, but not one of them has ever suggested this before.

"Why?" It's an honest question.

He shrugs. "Hard to picture you two apart."

I swallow. Gonna be hard to enjoy this soup and sandwich with a giant lump in my throat.

"Liv has her heart set on Vandy. She got her acceptance letter a few weeks ago." The pride in Matt's voice is palpable. Is it possible to get *two* lumps in one's throat?

"Wow, Liv." Clara's eyes widen, her voice ringing with sincerity. "That's impressive."

So is the bill. The lump in my throat swells like a grapefruit. I really should stop putting off the money talk with my parents, but then I overhear my dad whisper to my mom that he hopes we all remembered to order water. Like we don't already automatically know that—it's a reflex by now. His brows furrow as he presses his lips together in a thin line. Not good.

Matt, Clark, and Clara excuse themselves after lunch and head back to their respective schools. They don't miss much—we lose our second game in penalty kicks. A bit anticlimactic after the first go-round. I would never mention this to my teammates, but I'm a tiny bit relieved we don't have to stick around for a third game. It was hard to focus on the second after the lunch conversation and I have two quizzes at school tomorrow, plus a shift at work afterwards.

"Win some, lose some." Dad squeezes my shoulder and grabs my bag, then sticks it in the trunk again. He drives while mom helps me study for the assessments tomorrow, then chats with dad after we finish. It's sweet how they always hold hands on long car rides. And short car rides. All the time.

I'm tempted to doze off once the sun sets and the car grows dark, but a notification on my phone lights up the backseat. It's a calendar reminder that the Wonderbrink application is due this week. I rest my head against the seatback, unsettled. Did someone turn up the heat back here?

A second ping from my phone gives me something else to think about. It's a Core Four group text:

> Amber: How did our favorite soccer player do today?

> Tyler: I used to play soccer…

> Amber: (*edited to*) How did our favorite female soccer player do today?

> Tyler: Better.

> Me: We won our first game and I had an assist. We lost the second in penalty kicks. Womp Womp.

Xavier: Atta girl. Nice.

Amber: We watched The Goonies and both the guys fell asleep. I painted my toes (and two of Tyler's 'cause I couldn't pick a color. And because he was snoring). Anyway, you didn't miss much.

So, they went for a classic without me. That stings, but I'll live. I wonder who got the tortilla blanket?

Tyler: WUT? *removes sock*

Xavier: But we missed you.

Me: Please send a pic of Tyler's partial pedi?!

Tyler: PINK?! How does one remove this hideous monstrosity? And Liv… did you just ask for a foot pic? Does someone have a fetish?

Amber: If you want to get technical the colors are Pink-A-Boo and Crimson Allure, and stop trying to make things weird.

Xavier: Aww, Tyler. I bet you look so stinkin' CUTE.

Tyler: :/

Me: You'll have to catch me up on the sermon tomorrow, too. Tyler, wear your slides in the morning…

I text Xavier separately.

Me: My brothers got to come to my game today and Matt brought a girl. Clara goes to Western and she said she really likes it.

Xavier: Way to go, Matt! Is this Clara chick hot?

Me: Xavier… seriously?

Ugh, boys. I think he's kidding, but I'm not going to ask.

Xavier: I'm jokin'.

Me: She plays soccer. She must be good, too. She's D1 on scholarship.

Xavier: Nice. Almost as cool as going to Vandy to study illustrative art.

Annnddd the yucky sentiments of panic and dread visit my stomach again. Someone should probably just forward their mail there. I send Xavier one last text to let him know I'll catch up more tomorrow and put my phone away for the rest of the ride.

Dad parks the car in the garage and I gather my things. "I think I'm just going to fix a ham and cheese sandwich for dinner. Can I shower and then eat in my room while I work on homework?"

"Sure, sweetheart. Are you feeling ok?" Mom's frown adds to my shame.

"I'm fine." I squeak, then feel worse since they spent

their entire Sunday with me and my soccer team, and here I am trying to escape. "I want to study a little more. Thanks for helping me in the car."

She nods, so I make myself a sandwich and go back to my room. The mess from earlier is not a welcoming sight, and it takes a solid twenty minutes to straighten everything up. I throw my sandwich in the trash because who can eat with this level of anxiety? The thought of shoving this thing down my throat... ew. Instead, it's straight to the shower. Not even my lavender body wash can calm my thoughts. I brush my teeth, lay out my clothes for the morning, and set an alarm on my phone. Then I sit at my desk, power up my Chromebook, and pull up the Wonderbrink website.

I open the Word document saved with my 500-word essay, based mostly on my conversation with Paul at the coffee shop and bits and pieces of information gleaned at the Sugar Shatterers meetings, and upload the file to the site. It takes less than five minutes to complete the remainder of the application.

Way too easy. Deception on the level I'm performing should at least cost me hours of my life. Bile rises in my throat and churns my stomach into a giant knot. Ditching the ham sammy was a way better idea than this. After one last peek at the "expected financial contribution" page on the Vanderbilt site, I slam my eyes shut and click submit.

"Thank you, Your application has been accepted" flashes across the screen.

Conviction is a big fan of instant gratification. I rest my forehead on my desk and sit like that for a long time before I can make myself get up and walk to my bed. Pippa is resting on the corner of my comforter and she whimpers at me. It's almost like she knows I've messed up, and a tidal wave of shame washes over me. I pull the covers up to my chin and stare at the ceiling fan.

Around and around, my eyes follow the blades of the simple machine until they roll in my head.

And then I stare at my clock.

And then the fan blades going around in circles for another hour or so, save for the occasional glances back at the clock.

Ugh.

Turns out I didn't need to set that alarm. After tossing and turning all night, my clock now reads 6:15 a.m. Time to get ready for school, and I haven't slept a wink.

Chapter 9
Flagrant Foul

This week passes in a blur. A guilt-induced haze of school, practice, work, and the occasional Spirit Week shenanigans thrown in for funsies. At least Xavier keeps the sticky notes coming in fourth period.

Monday, guilt at school followed by an uneventful guilt-ridden shift at work.

Tuesday, guilt at school, tacos with a side of contrition during family dinner, and then more guilt at soccer practice.

Wednesday, guilt at school and then at church, where my remorse is magnified and I suspect my friends can see the literal word written on my forehead.

Thursday, guilt at school, another short shift at work, and then overwhelming regret at soccer practice when Coach Lonnie gave me a bunch of funny looks. Can he tell something is up? Has he been talking about Vandy with dad? Or is he just concerned about my guilt-impeded performance?

And sleep? Forget it. Nighttime anxiety is a cruel companion that leaves nothing but dark shadows under heavy eyelids.

Which brings me to today, Friday, where my guilt is blissfully overshadowed by a raucous pep rally. Our band starts us off with a blaring rendition of the fight song so loud my pulse starts to pound along with the percussion section. Our cheerleaders tumble all over the place, and the chaotic noise only dies once Principal Dolan takes the stage to announce the basketball players. Amber and I yell until we're hoarse when Tyler and Xavier are called, then it's an early dismissal, ranking right up there with snow days and delays.

And now? I may have been dragging my tired bum all week, but adrenaline has me wide awake because it's game time. Excitement washes over me as we pull into the gym parking lot, my feet drumming against the floorboard. The theme of tonight's game is Superheroes. I'm wearing a full-on Wonder Woman onesie and Amber is dressed as Ruth Bader Ginsburg. We all have our champions.

The atmosphere in the gym is electric—filled with the buzz of an intense rivalry that has simmered for years and has been building up all week. The student section for the Cadiz Colonels appears as a giant blob of hunter green, while the Barkley Bobcats assume a more eclectic mix of Avengers, Paw Patrol figures, and various X-Men characters scattered throughout an otherwise red and black sea of fandom. Jimmy came dressed in solid brown from head to toe. I would ask what superhero resembles a giant dookie, but he also has artificial leaves hot glued in random places and keeps repeating "I AM GROOT!" every few minutes.

The hardwood court gleams under the bright lights, and sneakers squeak as the players warm-up. The casual observer might think I was watching a tennis match while the guys get ready to play. On the left side of the court, Paul, on the right, Xavier. Paul. Xavier. Paul. Xavier.

But then I catch some odd behaviors. Paul has on the same neon socks he wore to the last game I watched weeks ago, one yellow and one green, except the neon isn't quite as bright. Less glow, more dingy. He... he has washed them this season, right? Right?

It's hard to look away as I watch him insist on shooting the last shot of warm-ups, then seems to avoid stepping on the paint lines when he walks to the locker room with his team. He taps the overhang of the entryway exactly three times before going in, and when they announce the line-ups before tip-off, he taps the Cadiz logo on his chest every time they call a teammate's name. It's oddly fascinating and somewhat tragic to watch.

"Whoa," Amber murmurs, almost under her breath. "He really does have some issues, huh?"

"Seems like it." I sigh, but then the commentator starts announcing Barkley players, and we clap like crazy.

They take their positions on the court, and from the moment they tip the ball, it's evident this game will be a touch chippy. The Barkley Bobcats and the Cadiz Colonels have squared off plenty of times in years past, but tonight feels different. It feels personal.

Paul plays shooting guard for Cadiz, stalking the

court like a predator, eyes locked on Xavier. Why does it seem like he's trying to prove something? He's playing rough—instigating contact, sneaking in the occasional elbow, stepping on other players' feet—and it gives me a yucky feeling deep in my gut.

After one particularly venomous stare down from Paul to Xavier, Amber, dressed as the adorable Supreme Court Justice she aspires to one day be, turns to me and points the gavel she brought as a prop in the air. "Remember, on this court, as in life, it's not the size of the player, but the strength of their determination that matters. Play fair, respect the rules, and may the best team win!"

I lower her arm before she hurts someone with her gavel whacker. "Calm down, your honor. May Barkley win, and may Paul stop playing dirty."

"Yes, that too. Amen."

In the final seconds before the half, Xavier steals the ball and is out on a fast break. Paul chases him down the court, and as Xavier approaches the basket for a layup attempt, Paul grabs his jersey. He tugs just enough to disrupt his balance but not enough for the motion to be too obvious. Unless, of course, you're watching like an obsessed best friend.

Which I one-hundred percent am.

Xavier stumbles slightly and it throws off his shot. How did the refs not see that?

"BOO!" Amber yells, and several other fans follow suit. Jimmy yells, "I AM GROOOOOOTTT!!!" I frown, but chewing my nails will be tonight's coping mechanism of choice. I'll stay quiet. She turns to me. "Did you see that? That was worse than the cafeteria jungle scene in *Mean Girls*. Does your buddy Paul always ball like a wild animal?"

At her question, several of our classmates snap their heads my way. I put my hands up, palms out. "We're more like acquaintances." Nervous, awkward giggles spill out of me. I've got to get out of here, and popcorn sounds like a better plan than keratin. I make an about-face and slip off to the concession stand as the cheerleaders take the court for their routine. Meagan is waiting in line and I do a double take when I spot her. Most of her face is covered in sparkly lime glitter and her hair is sprayed green.

"Game's a bit intense, huh?" Her glitter sparkles when she talks.

"No kidding."

One of Meagan's classmates walks past the waiting line, points at me, and yells, "No fraternizing with the enemy!" My friend rolls her eyes.

"Does Paul always play so... aggressively?"

"To anyone who didn't know better, aggressive is probably the right word. I think he plays desperately. He's good, but I've seen his dad lose his mind if he plays less than great. Most people think Paul's a jerk, but he's trying to live up to an impossible standard."

"And Xavier's collateral damage?"

Meagan winces. "Whoever Paul guards at *any* game becomes collateral damage."

"So, you and Paul are pretty close?"

She snorts. "Once upon a time, yes. Now? No one is

close to Paul." There's so much sadness in her voice. She grabs her nachos and soda and I, my popcorn. "Later, Liv."

"See you at soccer."

That was certainly enlightening.

"Excuse me." I lift my bucket of popcorn as I pass Jimmy and make my way to Amber while the halftime clock ticks away.

"I AM GROOT." He either said "no problem" or prom-posed, there's really no way to know for sure. I admire his commitment, though.

At the start of the second half, Xavier stands at the top of the key, bouncing on the balls of his feet. The scoreboard reads Cadiz 34, Barkley 32. We're down, but barely. The third quarter is much like the first half: intense.

When the fourth quarter starts, Xavier wipes the perspiration from his brow, then looks to steady his breath as he jogs back on defense. The minutes pass so quickly, my heartbeat can hardly keep up.

With little less than two minutes left, Cadiz is still ahead and every possession is a battle. Paul, living up to his ogre nickname, has been a thorn in Xavier's side all night. He drains shot after shot and has an answer for every one of our baskets.

There's less than a minute left now. The ball swings around to Xavier on the perimeter. He fakes a drive, then passes to Tyler, who's posting up in the paint. But Paul anticipates the play and lunges for the steal, his arm knocking the ball loose. Tyler dives to the floor, scrambling to regain possession, but Paul is faster. Amber growls as Paul snatches the ball and sprints toward the other end of the court.

Xavier chases him. As Paul approaches the three-point line, he hesitates. Xavier closes the gap and cuts him off. What happens next makes my heart stop in my chest. Paul does a spin move and drives hard to the basket while delivering an elbow into Xavier's ribs. Hard. The force sends Xavier crashing to the floor, then he grabs at his chest and groans. He's had the wind knocked out of him.

The ref's whistle shrieks through the chaos—loud and piercing—and echoes through the gym. Xavier winces, clutches his side, and tries to catch his breath. Paul stands over Xavier, chin high and nostrils flared. The ref hurries over, his face flushed. "That's a flagrant! You're outta here!" He points toward the locker room.

Paul's eyes grow wide. "What? That was clean!" His face twists in disbelief. He says something to Xavier, but I can't make out the words over the noise. He throws his hands up, but his coach grabs his arm and pulls him away from the court. I watch him disappear into the locker room. A few rows up from his departing form, I spot *Doctor Geoffrey Roberts, President of Bluegrass Baptist Health Hospital*, face red and arms crossed. Next to him sits a petite, well-dressed woman with a perfect high-lighted updo and an outfit entirely too proper for a high school basketball game. She's wringing her hands.

Yikes.

If I had to guess, I'd say that is his stepmom. How is it possible for me to be so annoyed with Paul yet worry for him at the same time? That ogre really is an onion.

As Xavier slowly gets to his feet and makes his way to the free-throw line Amber peels my fingers off her wrist. I guess I was a little anxious about the whole ogre-assaulting-my-bestie situation and went all death grip on her. Xavier plants his feet in a wide stance, bounces the ball twice, focuses on the rim, and sinks two in a row to tie the game.

With the clock winding down to the final seconds, Xavier takes control of the ball again. He drives down the court and weaves through defenders like they're standing still. He approaches the top of the key, finds an opening, and with a quick crossover, pulls up and launches a fifteen-foot jump shot.

The gym falls silent as the ball arcs through the air and spins toward the hoop. Time does that weird thing where it seems to stretch, then, with a soft swish, the ball drops through the net. The gym explodes into cheers so loud my ears hurt. Popcorn flies out of my bucket as Amber and I jump up and down. Jimmy yells "I AMMMMMM GROOOOOTTTTT."

When the final buzzer sounds, the score blinking on the board reads Barkley 64, Cadiz 62.

Xavier's rowdy teammates swallow him in a massive celebratory huddle and I lose sight of him for a moment. When they finally break apart to line up and shake hands with the other team, Xavier stands back, alone as he searches the crowd and his eyes lock with mine. He points at me, pats his chest, and winks.

This time, it's Amber who grabs a hold of my arm so tightly it's certain I'm going to need some Vaseline and a chisel to loosen her death grip. Did Xavier just...stake his claim on me? That whole chest tapping thing seemed like some Discovery Channel mating ritual. Was it supposed to communicate his feelings? Is this really happening?

It's going to be one heck of a wild ride to Comic-Con tomorrow.

Chapter 10
Never Meet Your Hero

I haven't been to Comic-Con since I attended eight years ago with Xavier, his dad, and his uncle. Hard pass on the costume this go-round, but my Guardians of the Faith sweatshirt and my cutest pair of jeans lay waiting on my bed. Cute fuzzy socks for the win, too. I throw on my clothes and braid my wild red curls into a fishtail. Lip gloss and mascara, and BAM, I'm good to go.

It's really happening. I'm actually going to meet *the* Paige O'Donnell today. In a matter of hours. All this anxious pacing is going to burn a path in my carpet, but what else am I supposed to do with all of this nervous energy until Xavier picks me up? Which is... now. Xavier is here now.

EEEEE, Paige O'Donnell, here I come. I grab my cross-body bag off the edge of my desk and fly from my room to the front door at a break-neck pace, then throw it open.

Oof. Hello pectoral muscles. I run smack into Xavier, whose arm is stretched toward the doorbell. When he covers my hand with his palm and grins, my brain forgets how to make words.

"Someone's excited." His brows raise and he gifts me an adorable, boyish grin. My hand is still on his chest, and his hand is still on mine. His heart beats steady in his chest. It's a good thing he can't feel my heartbeat picking up speed.

"You have no idea." Really, *no* idea.

"Do you have our tickets?"

I pull them out of my purse, fan them, then put them back.

"Your chariot awaits, passenger princess." He turns and gestures to his old Ford Ranger, breaking our contact. I open and close my hand several times—my right hand a tragic victim of instant withdrawal. My gallant knight opens the door for me and I slide across the soft, worn leather. The cab smells like a bakery and there's a folded bag from the Reyes Panaderya in the seat's center.

With the click of his seatbelt, he puts the truck in reverse, then motions to the bag. "Those pandesals won't eat themselves."

"Oh my gosh, pandesals, and Paige, and, and–"

"And Paducah rolled ice cream, oh my."

"Oh my, indeed." And because awkward silence is a fate worse than death, I broach the inevitable conversation. "That was some game last night, huh?"

He snorts, which is somehow cute when he does it. I sound like an asthmatic bear when I do that.

Except he stays quiet. "You okay?" Then, to get a rise out of him, I stuff a whole pastry in my mouth. If I can't talk, he'll have to.

"I don't get what you see in that guy, anyway?"

Alrighty then. We're talking about Paul instead of basketball. My stomach suddenly isn't so sure about the pastry.

"I–I think there's been a misunderstanding."

He grips the wheel with one hand and runs the other through his short, dark hair. "How so?"

"I don't like Paul that way. I'm not even sure I like Paul at all. He..." Why is it so hard to describe a non-relationship? What was it Meagan said about him? *No one gets close to Paul.* And I'm starting to think I don't want to anyway. "He doesn't seem like someone you can really get to know well. He's more like an acquaintance."

"I could have told you that. We played rec league ball together when we were younger and I tried to be friends with the guy, but..."

"But?"

"Something happened around middle school and since then, he doesn't do the whole friendship thing."

"Paul doesn't play well with others?" It's more of a statement than a question.

"Based on his ejection from the game last night, I'd say that's an understatement. I don't know what it is. He's too superstitious or too self-absorbed, too *something*."

"Sometimes I worry about him." I bite my lip, unsure of how Xavier will feel about that confession.

"I know you do, because you're a good person."

My cheeks warm at his compliment.

"I know you're a caring, sympathetic human being, but I'm glad you don't like him *"like that."*" He makes air quotes with his free hand. "He may have a reason for the way he acts, but you deserve better. Way better."

The air in the cab thickens and I have to look out the window so he won't see the tears threatening to spill from my eyes. I need a measure of courage so I can brave asking him about his gesture at the end of the game last night. I want to know if he likes me *like that* and not just as his best friend. But Paducah is still half an hour away, and that's too long to sit in miserable silence if I crash and burn.

I stuff another pandesal in my pie hole and turn up the country song so the twangy music can fill the empty space. Thank the Lord Xavier has a decent singing voice and can harmonize with the best of 'em.

When we pull into the convention center parking lot, there's a lot to take in. If my face matches Xavier's, my eyes must be bulging out of my head. Besides the costumes (So. Many. Costumes.) there must be hundreds of vendors and food trucks.

Drool.

We decide it's better to walk around outside to check out the merchants and offerings, then head in by noon for the Guardians of the Faith panel with Ms. O'Donnell.

People hawk books, jewelry, books in haphazard rows at some booths, fancy art supplies (more drool!), books displayed in stacks, comics, books on shelves, posters, and did I mention books... Holy Moly, look at that jewelry booth with gold necklaces and bracelets. Matt and Clark would love a poster from the booth near the entrance, and it's huge. It would be impossible to see everything, especially in one day. But I don't need to see it all. I want to listen to the panel with Ms. O'Donnell and then hopefully squeeze in a photo op at her table.

When we spot the Cluck Norris Turkey Truck, my jaw drops at the sheer size of the turkey legs passed off to the waiting customers. Oh my. They look golden and crispy in their greasy perfection. My mouth waters at the thought of how they might taste.

Xavier stops and, in his most solemn voice, declares, "We have to get one. For nostalgia's sake."

I take in the giant chunk of meat that surely contains enough steroids to make a celebrity testify to congress about roid rage, and turn to him. "You think I can eat one of those things?"

The cart guy calls out, "Nary a maiden too small for the mighty turkey leg!"

Xavier nods, already reaching for his wallet. "See. And eight-year-old you ate one. Don't be such a wuss."

My jaw drops and I make a face that I can only hope conveys my ire. He did *not* just call me a wuss.

Thirty super uncomfortable minutes later, I find myself jealous of anyone with an elastic waist band as part of their cosplay costume. I may never want food again. "Can you get a dolly and roll me to the podium?" I pat my protruding gut. "I'm having a food baby."

Bless his heart, Xavier blushes.

"Nah, we'll walk it off." He pulls up the conference center map on the conference app and studies it. "We've got half an hour until the panel, but we should get there early and get a good spot."

Say no more. There might be elaborate cosplayers all around me, but they're a fuzzy blur through my tunnel vision. When we get to Grand Ballroom 2B, the flood of Guardians of the Faith merch overwhelms me. Tables are cluttered with posters, clothing, and comics, and the crowds are so thick it's hard to walk. Up on the stage, there are five seats, four of which are occupied. In front of the empty seat, there's a name tag that reads "Paige O'Donnell."

"I bet she'll be here any minute," Xavier reassures me.

But as a worker delivers glasses of water to the other Guardians of the Faith authors and illustrators, they pass over her empty seat. The other panelists turn toward the front and appear to ready themselves for the event, and the surrounding crowd grows quiet in anticipation.

I try to keep my voice low, but I hate how whiny and disappointed I must sound to Xavier. "Maybe she's skipping the panel?"

"Figures." A man dressed as Mario mutters from somewhere behind me. "I can't believe she skipped out *again*."

"Just like L.A." His Luigi dressed friend clicks his tongue.

I pull at the end of my braid. O'Donnell got her big break in illustrative art when she signed with Guardians of the Faith, a Christian-based comic book. My grandparents had the Berenstain Bears, my parents had their Veggie Tales, and my generation? We got Guardians of the Faith. So... where is their illustrious illustrator?

Xavier's lips press together in a thin line, then he leans in close to my ear and puts a hand on the small of my back. "Let's get a head start to the table. Maybe we can catch her there."

We weave back through the crowded ballroom and sneak out the same way we came in. I grab us two bottles of water while Xavier consults the map again.

When we finally find her table ten minutes later, it's odd how her line is so short. And by short, I mean six people deep, measly compared to the lines wrapping around the other tables. This is insane. Paige O'Donnell is the premier artist in her field. She's won both an Eisner and a Harvey Award, and she's finaled in the Inkpot Awards. It's understandable that many fellow supporters may still be at the panel, but totally weird that her adoring fan base is, well, mostly me. A small group of teenagers blocks her from my view, and a person who appears to be an assistant sits to her left, head down. The teenagers leave, and now only a mom with her daughter separates me from my childhood hero—the woman whose talent inspired my love of art.

The mom's back goes ramrod straight, and she places her hand around her child. There are strong mama-bear vibes radiating off of her fuchsia cardigan. I watch as she turns, rolls her eyes, and marches her daughter away in a huff.

"Wait, you left your signed photo!" I reach for the picture but the mom responds, "Keep it."

Whoa, what? I watch as they stalk off. Is that little girl *crying?*

"Next." I look up and stare into the familiar face of

my childhood hero. Her curly blonde hair hangs loose in waves around her shoulders. My heart nearly beats out of my chest. I've rehearsed countless times what I wanted to stay in this moment. It'd be super if my hands could stop shaking. "Mrs. O'Donnell, it is a pleasure to meet you. I've followed your work for years. I've watched every interview and tutorial video you've ever—."

"Mmh-hmm. That's nice. Make this quick, kid. I've got a flight to catch in a few hours."

I freeze at the sharpness in her tone. "I just... I wanted to tell you that your work means a lot to me. I'm an artist too, and you're such an inspiration."

"Great. Keep practicing or whatever." The last part she mumbles. She flips open the top of a permanent marker, scrawls her signature on an eight-by-ten photograph, and shoves it across the table without so much as looking at me.

My throat tightens, and the words I'd rehearsed evaporate into stunned silence. Deep breath. "I-I was wondering if you had any advice for someone who wants to get into illustrative arts?"

Finally, Paige looks at me, her expression unreadable for a moment before she scoffs. "Advice? Sure, don't waste time at conventions like this. If you were a serious artist, you'd already know that."

Um, *she's* at this conference?

"Donkey! I see you met my aunt Paige." Paul drops a fresh mountain of eight-by-tens next to her and my jaw hits the floor.

AUNT Paige? Could this get any worse? And did Xavier just growl? My bulging eyes volley back and forth between Paige and Paul. Same green irises, same curly blonde hair, same indifferent expression. Now I see it. She looks like the female, slightly younger version of Paul's dad. Paige must be *Doctor Geoffrey Roberts, President of Bluegrass Baptist Health Hospital's* little sister. Well, I bet that makes for one heck of a fun-filled family dinner.

"Paul, I've got photos to sign. Can you please get your little friends away from my table?"

Except I'm rooted in place. And she most certainly does not have any photos to sign. Xavier and I are the only ones in line and you couldn't pay me to take one—and that's saying something. My hero has been reduced to a distant, disinterested figure. The pedestal I'd put her on crumbles.

Xavier pushes lightly against my back, encouraging me to walk away. "Let's just go, Li—"

"Told you I knew a famous illustrative artist, Donkey." Paul smirks. Am I supposed to be impressed by that information after meeting her? And "infamous" is much more fitting.

Xavier snaps. "Funny how you keep calling her 'Donkey' when you're the one who always seems to be acting like an as—"

"Xavier." His name grinds through my clenched teeth. This isn't like him.

He huffs, but refuses to break eye contact with Paul. "Do you even know her real name?"

"Paul." Paige's impassive tone grates. "Move."

Not that I wouldn't rather be anywhere else than right here, right now, but it is so tempting to point out that there are approximately zero ravenous fans in line behind us. Apparently, Paige's rude reputation has made the rounds. My former hero is not who I thought she was.

Paul studies my face for a mili-second. "Of course I know her name. Liz, right? Short for Elizabeth, I bet." He offers a proud smile I might have once found dazzling, but now it comes across as pretentious and cocky.

Get me out of here.

Xavier grabs my hand and gives it a healthy squeeze. He then stares directly into Paul's soul. "Are you ready to leave, *OLIVIA*?"

Paige heaves out a sigh and bangs her palms against the table, spilling the photographs in a half-hazard heap. "I've tried to be fair to you creatures, but now my patience has reached its end!" Is *she* seriously quoting *Shrek* now? She lifts a hand and shoos us away.

The unsanctified part of me would love to kick both of them in the shins, sans shin-guards, and run away like a petulant five-year-old. Xavier saves me from myself and—still holding my hand—pulls me toward the exit.

He doesn't let go in the parking lot, either. He stops abruptly and turns to face me. His tense jaw relaxes only when he lets out a deep sigh. "Listen, I'm sorry about Paige."

I want to say, "me too," but the words stick in my throat. No point in making Xavier feel bad. "It was a really thoughtful Palentine's Day gift, though."

He smiles at that, then opens the truck door for me. "You know what we should do now?"

"Drown our misery in rolled ice cream at Craving the Curls?"

"That's exactly what we should do." He puts the key in the ignition and the engine roars to life. "And I've got something I want to talk to you about."

Good gracious. I'm going to need this talk to be about the weather or politics, otherwise my brain might explode after the day I've had.

Chapter 11
Burrito Babe Burned

I'm not sure what Xavier wants to talk about, but it's not going to happen. As soon as he puts the truck in drive, I rest the back of my head against the headrest and a somber wave of *oh-crap* hits me, then the waterworks start. More like a slow trickle than a gushing waterfall, but still.

What have I done? I intentionally applied for a scholarship I'm in no way eligible for to attend a school my family absolutely cannot afford and I'm not even sure I even want to go anymore. Nothing against Vandy—it's an amazing school—but I have NO interest in following in that horrible woman's rude footsteps. My best friend paid for tickets and drove me an hour away to meet her, only to find out she's a punk and her nephew is an ogre, figuratively speaking. AND, I love said best friend. I have the pluck to apply for a scholarship I'm unfit for, but not enough bravado to tell him I caught the feels for him.

With that final thought, the tears fall with a little more gusto.

One thing I appreciate about Xavier is that a crying girl has never been something that freaks him out. I don't know if it's because he has sisters or maybe he's just more sophisticated than my brothers. He could be used to it since I'm a sentimental schmalz and tear up at every sappy movie we've ever watched.

Oh, who am I kidding? I've seen my dad cry and it totally freaked me out.

"I was so excited to meet her." Hiccup. "She's been my idol for years, and she just..." Hiccup. "...She brushed me off like I didn't matter." Hiccup. "She didn't even look at me when I said..." Hiccup. "... How much she inspired me." Oh good grief. My voice breaks on the last word and I cover my face with my hands. He stays still, giving me space to let the waterworks flow. Xavier listens intently, his expression calm but concerned. He doesn't interrupt, doesn't fidget, doesn't flinch. I wish my hiccups would take note.

"You looked up to her, and she let you down. Don't you think that says more about her than it does about you? You're an amazing artist and an even better person. If she couldn't see that, it's her loss. And for what it's worth," he adds with a playful grin, "her art is kind of overrated anyway."

I snort through my tears, half-laughing. "Uh, no." Hiccup. "It isn't. She might be rude, but her work is top notch."

"Psh." He slows the truck to stop for a traffic light. "Yours is better."

When I sniffle again, he reaches over with his free arm and gives my hand a little squeeze, a small smile on his lips. In a low voice, he reassures me, "It's ok if you're not up for ice cream. We can go home if you'd rather."

"What?" Sniff. "No." I grab a napkin leftover from breakfast and wipe under my eyes so I don't look like a splotchy raccoon. "You love ice cream and we're doing this."

"Ice cream will definitely help you forget Paige and Paul and—"

"Who?"

He grins at my question and that helps dry up any remaining tears. Quiets my hiccups, too. Is it too much to hope that ice cream will get the foul taste of Comic-Con out of my mouth?

We park on a cobbled side street near the river and walk into a shop with a cute black-and-white striped awning. The name Craving the Curls is painted in pretty font on the squeaky clean, sparkling windows. Xavier's told me about this shop before, but his description didn't do it justice. It's like walking into a cozy nook after the hustle and bustle of Comic-Con. And no one looks like a Klingon here, so that's a plus. The old, exposed brick walls add a rustic charm to the space. They're worn but well-kept, and they give the shop a sense of timelessness. It's warm inside too, and I run my hands over my arms in appreciation of the cozy atmosphere. It's especially nice since we're here to eat a frozen dessert in March.

Behind the counter, a beautiful woman whose name tag reads *Tanya* smiles at us. "Hey, y'all. What can I get you guys?" Her charm and charisma put me at ease instantly.

Xavier practically bounces on his toes. He's *giddy*.

"I'd love an order of S'mores please. NO–wait. Peanut butter brownie. No, no. Sorry. I'm *sure* I want an order of The Parent Trap. Oreos and peanut butter mixed with vanilla ice cream... oh man." He rubs his hands together. I have to stifle a smile. He's adorable when he's among his ice cream.

Her friendly face turns to me. "And for you?"

I chew my lip. There are so many delicious options. "I'd like an order of S'more's, please." I'll just share so he can try mine and get a variety. Tanya smiles like she knows what I'm up to and rings us up.

We watch in awe from behind glass panels as she and another worker pour cream on chilled slabs and work to roll the mixture into curls. She adds the other ingredients and continues her work. It's a labor of love. When she adds the marshmallow cream to the top of my curls and torches it, I grasp Xavier's elbow with excitement. Tyler would love this part. Maybe a little too much...

She grabs spoons then hands us our creations. "For the adorable couple."

"Oh, no, we're just—"

"Don't correct the nice lady, Liv. We are adorable." Xavier offers Tanya a charming smile and takes his cup.

We sit on padded stools, flush with a wooden table edge that protrudes from the wall. Our knees bump against one another—we're so close. The fare is so yummy we barely speak for a solid five minutes, content to fill our bellies. Again. The communication during our dessert is mostly "mmmm..." or "so good," except for the three times Xavier asks if he can have a bite of mine.

When we're finished, Xavier throws our cups in the trash and we push in our seats. I wait for Xavier to reach for my hand... I half expect him to after he basically agreed to Mrs. Tanya's "adorable couple" comment, but he doesn't. Can he not sense the elephant in the room? Is that what he wanted to talk about? I don't want to ruin this moment, so I'm not going to bring it up if he doesn't.

Call me a coward, but I pretend to fall asleep on the way home, satisfied to enjoy the hum of the engine and Xavier occasionally singing along to his playlist. He's surprisingly good. When he pulls into my driveway to drop me off, I wait until he gently nudges my shoulder to pretend to wake up. My yawn, though, that's genuine. When I peel my eyes open, the twilight pink sky makes for a stunning backdrop against my small home.

Xavier keeps the truck in park and the engine quietly purrs. "Listen, Liv. I know today didn't work out like you'd probably hoped, but don't let that take away the joy you feel when you make art. You've got a gift."

There it is again—my throat grows tight and I bite my lip. "I won't." It comes out as barely a whisper.

He nods as I help myself out. "Night, Liv."

"Good night."

He stays parked until I'm safely inside, then puts the truck in reverse. I watch from the window as his headlights skid across the trees lining the driveway, then disappear down the road.

* * *

Ah yes, sleepless night number six in a row. Guilt keeps the sandman away, and this morning is another uneventful culmination of eight hours lost. There's a guest missionary speaking at church today, and though I'm super into his message, when we bow our heads to pray at the conclusion of the service, Xavier startles me when he loudly clears his throat. I guess my head drooped onto his shoulder just before the "Amen."

Amber doesn't look much better than I feel, which is exhausted. She's as pale as a ghost and she's hardly said a word all morning. As we head to the foyer to make our way to the parking lot, Xavier's mom stops us.

"Babae! Are you well? Come here and let Mama Reyes take a look at you." Half a dozen bracelets jingle down her thick arm as she places the backside of her hand against Amber's head and frowns. "Oh, babae. Tyler, you bring your kasuyò by our house and I'll get her some sopas. And she needs some rest." As if to prove her right, Amber sneezes and lets out a little groan. My poor friend.

I give her a little rub on the back. "Feel better soon, friend." She barely nods. Thankfully, Tyler is in full-on protective boyfriend mode. He's already pulled up the closest pharmacy on his phone and has asked twice if she prefers ibuprofen or acetaminophen. I have no doubt he'll do exactly whatever Mrs. Reyes suggests.

Our movie afternoon was supposed to be spent at Amber's, but considering she's got the crud, Xavier and I pick up burgers on the way to his house and end up in his living room instead. We pull into a spot on the street as Tyler exits the back door, a to-go cup of hot broth in his hand. He gingerly hands it to Amber, who is waiting in the passenger's seat, slumped against the window.

I love Amber and hate that she's probably got a serious NyQuil nap in the near future, but her and Tyler's absence means I get the coveted tortilla blanket all to myself. Always look for the silver lining. And since I get the blanket, Xavier gets to pick the movie. Which is probably good, since I'm sure he'll pick a masculine man movie and I won't have to worry about watching a rom-com alone with my boy bestie.

He picks *Top Gun: Maverick*. Perfect.

After we finish off our lunch, we grab popcorn and two glasses of water, then make ourselves comfy. Xavier leans back with my tortilla-trapped feet in his lap. His right hand rests on my ankles and he drapes his left casually over the back of the sofa.

Tom Cruise fills the screen, taking a military jet to extreme speeds. I sense Xavier isn't looking at the TV–I can feel his gaze on me. "Why are you staring at me?"

"You're a burrito babe." He motions to my auburn locks. "With some wild hot sauce on top." His crooked grin could cook this burrito.

I scrunch my nose as my cheeks flame. "I'm not a babe, you weirdo."

He chokes out a laugh. "You question the fact that I called you a babe, but not a burrito? Who's the weirdo?"

I laugh, but as soon as it spills out of me, a crushing weight squeezes my lungs. The heaviness of my secret gnaws at my insides.

Nothing gets past my friend. "Hey, you okay?" Xavier's brows furrow and his easy smile falters, replaced with concern. He sits up straighter, studying my face. "You still bummed about yesterday?"

"No. Well, sort of." Gulp. "There's something I need to tell you."

"Same. We didn't talk at Craving the Curls yesterday like I thought we might. We were too busy enjoying cryogenic ice cream and then you conked out on me." He picks at a thread on the edge of the tortilla blanket and starts moving his thumb in small circles over the cuff of my fuzzy sock.

I swallow hard, my heart hammering. It's too hard to meet his eyes. "I messed up."

"Okay..." His tone shifts, more cautious now, like he can sense the seriousness of my situation. "What kind of messed up? Like, you scratched your car on a mailbox or you need help hiding a body? I just need to know what we're working with here."

I wiggle my hands free from the blanket, stretch my fingers out, and pull the edge of the fabric to my chin. "You know how I met Paul at the diabetes support group?"

His hand freezes and he tenses up at the mention of my acquaintance. "Yeeahhhh. You told me something about making flyers for their fundraiser."

"I am..." I close my eyes and force myself to keep going. And then I tell him. Everything. It spills out of me like word-vomit, and once I start, it's impossible to stop. I share how I first learned about the Wonderbrink scholarship the day I met with Mrs. Carlson during my senior guidance check-in. How I read about the Sugar Shatterers on the Wonderbrink Website and checked it out after the disastrous dinner with my brothers. About how I was thrilled to be accepted into Vandy, then the desperation I felt after seeing that stupid "expected family contribution" page.

How it was like mourning the death of a dream. I even tell him how I asked Mr. Winters to write a letter of recommendation. And, worst of all, I tell him how much I dislike myself because everything is my fault and I should have just talked to my parents. I'm angry because I ruined his perfect Palentine's Day gift when I elevated Ms. O'Donnell to unhealthy, unrealistic expectations and planned my future based on her past. What a stupid, stupid thing to do.

"I'm especially sorry I kept so much from you," I finish, my voice hoarse from my confessional.

Xavier sits frozen, his gorgeous face a mixture of confusion and hurt. "You did all that, then hid it from me —from everyone—for two whole *months*?" His voice grows tighter as the hurt seems to sink in.

I flinch at his question. "I'm so sorry I didn't tell you. It's so dumb now, but I was desperate. I was afraid of losing out on my stupid dream school. But now I'm more afraid I'm going to lose you." My voice wobbles on the last few words.

His jaw clenches as he looks away, his fingers tapping against the edge of the couch as he processes my words. "Liv, we're supposed to tell each other everything. We always have. I would've told you if it were me. I don't get why you didn't trust our friendship enough to confide in me."

I stiffen, angry heat surging through my body. "How

can you know that?" I snap. "You're going to Murray as a Regent Scholar, no sweat. You've never known the strain of living low income or doing without. You don't need a part-time job, whereas I have to hoard every penny I make at Grace & Glimmer to save up for school. You have a financially secure family. I don't. We may be better off than we used to be, but I know my parents' bank account is stretched to the max with my two brothers at college and me on the way. Lord willing."

He runs a hand through his hair and lets out a bitter laugh. "Seriously? Pastoring isn't the most lucrative job on the planet. Neither is owning a restaurant, where I *work*, I might add. You make it sound like I don't appreciate what I have."

I shut my eyes, trying to hear myself as he did. Crap. "You're right. I didn't mean to make it sound that way."

"A diabetes scholarship? Geez, Liv. I can't believe you would do something like that. I wish you would've told me before you applied. I would've tried to talk you out of it."

"So do I. I was scared, okay?" I try to sit up but this dang burrito is tight. Tears threaten to spill over as my chest tightens. "I know I messed up. I should have told you guys, but I didn't want to ruin the Core Four, and especially not my friendship with you."

Xavier pinches the bridge of his nose and, after what feels like an eternity, finally speaks again, his voice quieter, "You're my best friend, Liv. I guess I didn't think you'd keep something like that from me."

That does it. That's the tipping point. My tears spill over, and I swipe at them. "I'm so sorry, Xavier."

Because Xavier's as kind as I am awkward, we sit like that, stiff and fearful, silent for a solid ten minutes before I can't take it anymore.

"I think maybe you should take me home, Xavier." I choke back my sniffles and try to stay composed. "Or I can call my parents since I'm guessing you'd probably rather not."

I bend my wrapped-up knees as much as I can so Xavier can stand. He shoves his hands into his pockets as he takes a few steps away. His shoulders are tense, and he seems to be struggling to find the right words. He turns back to me, his face softer, but the hurt in his eyes breaks my heart. "You don't have to leave, Liv," he says quietly. "I just... I can't figure out why you didn't trust me."

Just rip my heart out and stomp on it at this point. "I'm sorry, Xavier. I'll get my things, okay?"

Except it's quite difficult to unwrap from a burrito state and keep what's left of one's dignity, proven by the fact that I roll off the couch with an unceremonial thunk as I attempt to do so. When I finally struggle free and make it up from the floor, Xavier is staring at the carpet, refusing to make eye contact. He carries my bag and walks me to the door.

The ride home is the longest, most uncomfortable seven minutes of my life. Xavier's resting his chin on his closed fist, elbow on the window seal. When I climb out of his truck, I don't even tell him goodbye. What am I supposed to say? *See you tomorrow!* Uh-uh.

And school Monday? The thought of facing my friends sounds miserable. I've got an overwhelming urge to make this right *immediately*. But since I can't, it'll be another sleepless night. I've got to speak to Mr. Winters first thing in the morning.

When I open the door and start to remove my shoes, I hear my mom on the phone with someone. "Yes, Vanderbilt! We're so, so proud of our girl."

Chapter 12
Confession Time

The loudspeaker crackles to life, echoing down the hallway with an early morning announcement. "Oliva James to the front office, please." I straighten. That's got to be a record. I haven't even made it to first period. I finish stuffing my backpack into my locker, check the locker mate mirror—yep, those giant black circles are still under my gritty eyes—and grab my binder and Chromebook, then head that way.

When I round the corner, Mom is sitting in a chair outside of the guidance suite, legs crossed the same as her arms, her face a shade of red so dark it blends into her auburn hair.

That can't be good.

"Mom? What are you doing here? Is everything ok?" As dad isn't sitting beside her, a terrible thought overcomes me and the blood drains from my face. "Did something happen to dad?"

"Your father is fine. He couldn't get off work with such short notice. Olivia Mae James, help me understand why I've been called to your school this morning. Mrs. Carlson mentioned something about a missing scholarship document? I'm confused. Surely you understand the importance of scholarships at this point."

A missing scholarship document? What? And great, the whole name. This might be a fate worse than death. Cold dread washes over me and I slide down limp in the open seat next to her. "Momma, I think we need to talk."

Based on my mom's slack-jaw reaction, she wasn't expecting me to say that. "Yes, we do."

"Mrs. James, Olivia, you can come in now." Mrs. Carlson is standing at the door to her guidance office in front of a seated Mr. Winters. My mom takes a seat as well. Since those were the only two chairs in her small office, I elect to stand.

Do I really have to do this all over again after yesterday? Mrs. Carlson stays silent, but Mr. Winters does not. "Olivia, can you tell me what this is?" He holds in his hand a torn open envelope with a gold seal embossed on the back.

I swallow. "Yes sir, that appears to be a letter from the Wonderbrink Society."

"You are correct. You asked me to write a letter of recommendation for a Wonderbrink scholarship and indicated me as your reference on their website. This," he holds up the tattered paper, "is a reminder that your application is incomplete, save for my recommendation."

"Oh, thank God," I whisper. My shoulders sag as relief courses through me. My head relaxes back against the books stacked on Mrs. Carlson's office built-ins. All three adults stare at me now. It seems they weren't expecting me to say that. Mom blinks rapidly, she seems even more confused now than before.

Mr. Winters clears his throat. "Interesting. Olivia, I was honored when you asked me to write a letter. You're one of my best students. You're a hard worker, you've always had a great attitude, and you have stellar grades. But when I looked up this foundation, I knew I couldn't write the recommendation. I need you to explain why you asked me for a letter of rec for a *diabetes* scholarship?"

Mom's face morphs from red to ashen and she grabs her armrest with white knuckles.

The exhaustion, the weight of the guilt... they've had their way with me and it's all caught up, culminating in this moment. So, here it goes. "Because I got into what I thought was my dream school—spoiler alert, it's not. But then I saw the *expected family contribution* and let me tell you, I can either go to Vandy and live a life under the weight of crushing debt, or buy a private island and live out the remainder of all my friendless days there. When I saw that scholarship on Mrs. Carlson's desk, I got crazy desperate because I don't really aspire to be a parasitic leech on my parents, so—long story short—I applied."

Tears blur my vision, but I keep my focus on the diploma's hanging on the wall behind Mrs. Carlson, unwilling to make eye contact with anyone. Deep breath, and then I continue. "Hindsight's twenty-twenty, but believe me, I know exactly how idiotic that idea was. I'm glad you didn't write the letter, Mr. Winters. I mean, how awkward would it have been if I'd actually completed the application and then won, am I right?" Psychotic, maniacal laughter fills the space around me, then I realize that noise is coming from me. It's like a rancid cherry on top of curdled ice cream.

Mrs. Carlson covers her gaping mouth with one hand, the other falls lame into her lap. Mr. Winters may need to push his eyes back into their sockets once he picks his jaw up off the floor. Mom massages her temples as if an Olivia induced migraine is in full force. Guilt twists my stomach, and then terror, when she claps her hands in her lap and targets me with an eye-blazing glare.

"Olivia," she grinds through her teeth, enunciating each syllable as if it pains her. "As fun and mortifying as this little meeting has been, your father and I want you to be happy and your education is important to us. Sure, a scholarship would be amazing, but we're not struggling quite as bad as you seem to believe. Even if we were, I really, really wish you would have talked to us about this."

I lean back against Mrs. Carlson's bookshelves again, defeated and thoroughly drained. "Me too."

"Is there anything else you'd like to add, Olivia?" Somehow Mrs. Carlson's patient voice is full of undeserved grace.

"Yes." And then it's all eyes on me. "I'm sorry to all of you." My eyes pool and I blink away tears. Mr. Winters offers a small, merciful smile. "I'm sorry for putting you in that position, Mr. Winters. And I'm sorry I didn't ask more about alternative scholarships, Mrs. Carlson."

"And?" Mom snaps.

"And I'm sorry for disappointing you and being deceitful."

"And I'm sorry to inform you that you're grounded for the foreseeable future. You'll go to soccer or work, then straight home for homework and chores. If you're home, your phone will be with me or your father."

"Yes, ma'am." I give a contrite nod.

Mrs. Carlson pushes her glasses up. "Olivia, you applied to schools using the common application, correct?"

Mrs. Carlson's question catches me off guard. "Um, yes ma'am."

"Good girl. Let's schedule another meeting later this week and figure out a new plan." She scribbles out an excuse note. "Right now, you need to get to first period."

My mom, queen extraordinaire of hugging, stays stoic in her chair. "Straight home after school, young lady."

I take my note and nod as I exit.

Since Amber's home with the flu, my morning classes are uneventful. I'm not sure if Xavier told her or Tyler about what I did, but I eat lunch at one of the tables outside, alone. I suffer through the cold and decide being chilly is a fair consequence for my shameful deeds. Penance requires a jacket and is served with a side of soggy peanut butter and jelly.

I will not be a chicken heart. I will go to fourth period and I will sit in my chair and I will try to learn something. Except it turns out it's not that easy. I squirm in my seat under Mr. Winter's scrutiny—at least that's how I perceive it. I can't even bring myself to look the man in the eyes. The hardest part of the whole fifty-five-minute class period is resisting the urge to interact with Xavier and figure out where his head is. At least it's Motivational

Monday and Mr. Winters is showing *Inside Out*. We've got a discussion guide and everything, but I don't get a sticky note today, and that breaks my heart. I could play Sadness' role to a T.

When the lights come back on and Mr. Winters instructs us to put our worksheet away for next week, Xavier is quick to jump up and rush out the door. When he brushes past Tyler in the hallway, our friend watches Xavier's brisk retreat down the hall, then turns his face toward me. Tyler's eyebrows squish together and he has a big, uncharacteristic frown on his face. "What movie did y'all watch yesterday, *Schindler's List?*"

I lean against the lockers and let out a heavy sigh. The truth shall set me free. "I confessed to telling a lie and he's upset with me."

Tyler's face goes slack. "What?"

"I messed up. I wasn't honest with Xavier about something pretty important. Yesterday I fessed up."

He rubs his brow as if I'm giving him a migraine too—it's an Olivia epidemic. "I understood that part. What did you lie about?"

Might as well say it. "A diabetes scholarship."

"Uh... Okay?"

My shoulders slump. "I haven't been honest about it with anyone in the Core Four lately, and I'm so, so sorry." My chin does that weird quivery thing it likes to do when I try not to get emotional. It isn't working. At his bewildered expression, I collect my things and get ready for fifth period. "Tell Amber I said hi and I hope she feels better. Bye, Tyler."

"Liv, wait!" He catches up with me and reaches for

my arm. "I bet it took guts to confess that. You and Xavier will figure it out. You guys just need to talk."

"Really? That didn't work so well yesterday."

"I'm right, and I know it. I'd bet this week's paycheck on it." He's got a gleam in his eye and his shaggy, dusty brown hair moves as he tilts his head back, chin up.

I hope he's right.

* * *

I'm granted furlough for soccer, and it's amazing how well I can play when I've got pent up anxiety and angst to let loose. We circle up to stretch before practice ends, and the relief that I don't have to apologize to anyone here is marvelous.

"Way to work, woman. Friday's game inspire you?" Meagan gives me a playful swat as she reaches for a towel. Coach Lonnie blows his whistle, and we reach down to stretch out our calves.

"Ha, hardly. That game was... something."

"Paul is *still* griping about that flagrant foul." She rolls her eyes. "*Paul* is flagrant."

"Do you ever worry about him? Or wonder why he treats people like they're... they're..."

"Disposable?" Meagan lifts a brow. Or is it lowers a brow? Our heads bob upside-down, so maybe it doesn't matter.

I shut my mouth. Disposable is actually the perfect word for it. "Yeah. I thought we could be friends, but I'm pretty sure that's not a good idea."

The whistle sounds again and we switch to a standing hip flexor pose.

"I'm sorry." She winces. "He used to be such a nice guy. His dad is just so intense with the pressure and after his parents divorced, his superstitions went next level severe. He lost a lot of friends because of it, yours truly included. It's kind of a shame and... I miss him sometimes. The old Paul, I mean." Meagan's cheeks pinken, and I don't think it's because our heads are still inches from the floor. "I think his stepmom might be a good influence, though."

The whistle interrupts us and we shift into dog-facing-forward, my favorite.

"We can hope, I guess."

"Have you talked to him since Friday?"

I snort. "Yep. I ran into him when I was with Xavier at Comic-Con to meet Paige O'Donnell."

"Aw, she's your art hero, right? Was it amazing?"

"She's Paul's aunt. And she's been downgraded to 'villain' in my story."

Meagan freezes. "That stinks. Didn't see that coming."

"Yes, it does." I sigh. The final whistle blows in two short bursts, signaling it's time to huddle up. We break with our standard "FAMILY ON THREE!" chant, and it's back to prison for me.

But prison isn't quite the cold penitentiary I expect. My dad is waiting on the couch in the living room when I pass from the kitchen on the way to my room. He pats the seat next to him. "We need to talk."

Actually, prison might be preferred to this. I can't bear to break my father's heart.

"Your mom filled me in on your, eh, situation."

I nod, because what can I say to that? The best I've got is, "I'm sorry, Daddy." So that's what comes out of my mouth.

He gives me a small smile, and I'm crushed by the sadness behind it.

"I'm disappointed because I know you're capable of being honest, even in tough situations. I know how much you have your heart set on Vanderbilt. Liv, If you're worried about something, *tell us*. Your mother and I love you, and we want you to trust that we can face things together."

My chin starts to tremble again and dad pulls me into a crushing hug. "This doesn't change how much we love you or believe in you. We're going to work on rebuilding trust together."

"I don't know how to make this right." Can a girl dehydrate from too many tears?

"Do you still want to go to Vandy?"

"I don't know," I whisper.

"Your mom said you're worried we can't afford it."

"Can we?"

Dad releases me, then leans forward and puts his hands on his knees. "You know how your mom sometimes teases me about my frugal ways? She'll use little terms of endearment, like... Rebate Ranger, or Tightwad Tyrant?"

A smile pulls at my lip. "I prefer Dollar Defender or Savings Samurai myself."

He chuckles. "When your mom and I first got married, we were poor as dirt, but rich in love. Neither one of us came from much, but we work hard and we've always gotten by. I don't regret not talking about our financial situation with you more...you're our *child*, what kid needs that burden?" He takes a deep breath and massages his temples. "Listen Liv, college might come with massive sticker shock, but nobody said it was all due at once. If you truly want to go to Vandy, we'll figure something out. Even if that means helping you pay off loans after you graduate. Okay?"

I nod, because that's a lot to process and I'm not really sure what to say.

"Now, about this diabetes scholarship..."

My gaze snaps back to his face.

"I'm guessing your mother has already read you your rights."

"Sir, yes sir." I hand over my phone.

When he smiles again, there isn't so much sadness anymore. "We'll get through this, Liv. You're still my girl."

I give him another hug, then make my way to my room for homework and retribution.

My favorite part of Tuesday is that I don't have any earth-shattering confessions to make. Assuming dad talked to Coach Lonnie, anyone who matters or needs to know already does. I go to school, go to work, and go home. Same thing Wednesday, except I go to soccer and church instead of Grace & Glimmer. No sticky notes, and the world keeps turning while I'm at home scrubbing toilets or vacuuming. Or dishes. Or dusting. Oh, and homework.

It's Thursday and I'm expecting more of the same, except Amber's back. Her skin is still pale and her eyelids seem to hang like tired curtains over her bloodshot eyes, but she's back.

I offer her a sympathetic smile. "The flu sounds awful. I'm sorry."

"It doesn't sound as bad as liabetes. Tyler said you and Xavier have been avoiding each other all week."

Liabetes? Really?

When I tear up, she puts her things on the floor and pulls me into a tight hug. "I'm only teasing about the liabetes. I'm sorry you didn't think you could talk about it with us."

When she lets go, I rub my palms under my wet eyes. "Why are you apologizing? Liabetes is very clever. And justified." Can someone get me some tissues over here?

"So, um, just curious. Did you get any sticky notes this week?"

So, I'm not the only one alarmed by this. "Not a one."

Her shoulders sag. Why do the sticky notes seem as important to her as they do to me?

Amber taps her chin. "Do you work tonight? I have an idea."

"Yes ma'am, four to six, then I have soccer."

"Perfect. Bring the sticky notes you already have and your paint pens." Color is flooding back into Amber's animated face. She looks almost as giddy as Xavier did when we ordered ice cream at Craving the Curls.

Funny how that feels like a lifetime ago.

"But I'll be working? I can't paint and work the register at the same time." I don't need any other adults disappointed in me.

She whips out her phone and her fingers fly. "Okay. Tyler can take your shift. Do you think your mom would let me come over?"

"That's a no. I mean, I'm grounded."

"Liv," she scoffs, "Please. Your mom loves me." Her furious fingers work out another text before she shoves her phone in my face. "See? She said 'yes.'"

I grab the phone to examine it closer. "She did not." Except she did. Huh.

"It's 'cause I'm such a good influence. Way better than Paul." She says his name with such disdain that I flinch.

The two-minute warning bell rings and as we make our way to our first period classes, a sense of calm washes over me.

Thank God for best friends.

Chapter 13
Grace Upon Grace

Turns out, I did have to work last night. Amber shared her stomach flu with Tyler—Influenza Type Bae—and since he helped take such amazing care of nursing her back to health when she was sick, she's now playing the doting girlfriend and taking care of him. I was halfway through my shift when I got an email from Mrs. Carlson. She's scheduled a meeting for this morning to discuss my college options. Mid-March feels insanely, irresponsibly late to consider a potential college change, but here I am. She even assured me in her message that Commitment Day isn't until May first, so technically I have plenty of time. Maybe she's afraid I'll spazz out over the time crunch and apply to another scholarship I'm ineligible for.

That ain't happening.

Fortunately, since Amber couldn't come over yesterday afternoon, Mom agreed to let her spend the night tonight, so I have that to look forward to.

"You can come in, Olivia." This time, Mrs. Carlson

has a smile on her face, much more welcoming than the foreboding, grim line she wore Monday. I shudder just thinking about it.

I take my seat and set my backpack on the floor.

"Alrighty, then." She pushes her stylish turtle-shell readers up the bridge of her nose and glances at her computer screen. "How did the financial aid conversation about Vanderbilt go with your parents? Is Vandy still your top choice?"

"They assured me they can make it work if I want to go, but I'll be honest... it doesn't hold the same appeal as it used to."

She leans back in her chair. "Talk about that with me a bit. What's going on here?" She taps her temple.

I swallow. "Well. Vanderbilt is an amazing school, with an outstanding art program..."

"But?"

"But I wanted to go for all the wrong reasons and I'm mad at myself for what I did to try to make it work." I will hold it together. I will not cry. Repeat times one thousand.

"Humor me a bit and remind me of your back-up schools?"

"In Kentucky, Spalding and the University of Louisville both have strong art programs. In Tennessee, Lee and Sewanee are supposed to have good programs. I don't remember if Lee accepts the Common Application."

"Have you considered Berea? When you filled out your FAFSA, you automatically applied for the Pell Grant. I've heard they have an outstanding visual arts program."

I look up at the ceiling and blink back tears. I have to say it. I have to. "Be honest, Mrs. Carlson. Do you legitimately think I can still get into a respectable college for next fall? It's so late in the game. Should I consider a... a gap year or something?"

Mrs. Carlson clears her throat and starts reading from a shiny paper, "Berea College provides a work-study grant to cover all remaining tuition fees after subtracting the total sum accepted students receive through the Pell Grant."

My head snaps back to her face. She has a conspiratorial gleam in her eye. She returns her focus to the brochure in her hands. "Berea boasts bachelor's degrees in thirty-three majors. The college's mandatory work-study program requires students to engage in at least ten hours per week of work for the college."

"SHUT. UP." Thankfully, Mrs. Carlson is fluent in teen, otherwise I'm sure she'd be pretty upset with me for saying that. Still, her eyes grow wide as she glances over her readers and gleams. I reign in my enthusiasm and continue. "That was said with all the love of Jesus and excitement in my heart. Mrs. Carlson, I can totally work. I love working. Working is my favorite."

"I was hoping you'd say something like that. I've scheduled a meeting for you with an admission's counselor on Monday."

"Mrs. Carlson, am I allowed to hug you?"

She holds up a hand as I start to rise and I fall back into the chair. "Before you do that, I need you to promise me you'll really look at their website this weekend. Take this brochure, too. The counselor will expect to see your academic records, your test scores, all extracurricular activities, community service, the works. Most of that you've already included in the Common Application. But Olivia, you've spent so long laser-focused on Vandy, I'm worried you may have developed a little tunnel vision. Please make sure while you prepare for Monday, you're able to demonstrate a genuine interest in the college to their representative. Is that clear?"

"Yes ma'am, crystal clear. I won't let you down."

"I'm sure you won't."

"Mrs. Carlson?"

"Yes, dear?"

"Thank you." My voice breaks on the last word, but at least she lets me hug her before she sends me back to class. She writes my excuse note on a hot-pink sticky note.

Which only makes me think of Xavier.

My first instinct is to run straight to him and share this exciting news. But I can't. My mood's pendulum swings from riding high to majorly bummed so fast I may need to stop by the nurses office to get checked for whiplash.

Most of my peers are swimming in what one might describe as senioritis, but this Berea pamphlet has reignited my concentration. I keep pulling out my binder, looking it over, and putting it back again. Or I scroll through the college website. The campus is beautiful. There's a torrential downpour raging outside, so I soldier through lunch in the cafeteria for the first time all week. I even show the tract to Amber and notice Xavier peek out of his peripheral vision. He's not exactly giving me the silent treatment, but our conversations have been stilted and formal. I hate it.

When we get to fourth period, it's supposed to be Free to Learn Friday, but Mr. Winters is standing at his podium with a football. Did he change the theme to Football Friday? It's March, so who knows?

He clears his throat, then hesitates. Mr. Winters has never been one to hesitate, so I sit up a little straighter in my seat. This must be important.

"I thought we'd have a short discussion to start class off today." He rubs the back of his neck, then squares his shoulders. "You know, in a football game…"

Okay, this is so not what I expected. Based on the confused expressions of my classmates, neither did they.

"Close games are lost when receivers choose to look over their shoulders. Resist that temptation—it breaks your momentum going forward. Learn from your mistakes, sure, but forget what lies behind."

If he makes eye contact with me, I will spontaneously combust, I'm one-hundred percent certain of it.

Mr. Winters pinches the bridge of his nose. "I'm sorry guys, I feel like I'm messing this one up." He puts the football on his desk and picks up a well-worn book. "What I'm trying to say, Pastor Platt says better. Listen to these wise words from *Counter Culture*."

Jimmy pipes up while Mr. Winters flips to a dog-eared page. "Ain't you afraid you'll get fired for reading to us about that stuff?"

"I'm not grading you on whether you agree with me or not, son, and I'm only planning to read one paragraph. And I can't think of a better reason to get fired." Mr. Winters winks at Jimmy–*WINKS* at him—before returning to the passage.

"'God does not desire for you or anyone else to live with the pain of regret. It is altogether right to hate sin in your history. The pain of past sin is often a powerful deterrent to future sin, but don't let it rob you of the peace God has designed for you in the present. Remember what Jesus said to a woman who had lived an immoral lifestyle: 'Your sins are forgiven... Your faith has saved you; go in peace' (Luke 7:48–50). God desires that peace to be yours today... To all who trust in Christ, remember this...'"

He closes the book and the classroom remains silent. A pin drop might sound like an explosion the air is so still. He stares right at me for a millisecond, but it feels like much longer and energy vibrates through me.

"I've been a teacher for over twenty years, and I know it's cliche—heck, I probably said it last year and the year before that—but this group of seniors is special to me and I love you guys." If he starts to cry, every girl in this class is a goner. We're going to need more than one box of tissues. "You're about to graduate and I'm proud of you. I just wanted to share that little bit with you."

When the class continues to stay silent, he puts his hands up. "That's enough mush."

Is he serious? That *mush* was a great gift but it made my heart practically beat out of my chest.

"You guys enjoy Free to Learn Friday." What he

means is, we're free to work on anything we'd like. Study hall, knitting, juggling, underwater basket-weaving. He doesn't care, just learn something. I'm too scared to move while I continue to process what he read.

And then, Xavier scribbles out a message, no *TWO* messages on sticky notes and seals them to the corner of my desk. One has "I miss my best friend. Can we please talk?" The other has the number thirty-one in the top left and a large question mark in the center, both written in his charming, boyish handwriting.

The pendulum swings back. I'm going to need a giant nap when I get home from the emotional toll of this day. Also... not a letter on the sticky note this time, but punctuation. Interesting.

With a shaky hand, I grab my pencil and pause before I begin to draw. This is too important to take lightly.

I reach into my pencil pouch and take out the few paint pens I keep with me. I go hard-core on those sticky notes. Extravagant doodles that would make Michelangelo proud. Sam Cox would claim me as his protégé, I'm sure of it. Rembrandt would weep. *Weep!* Swirly-swirls, zentangles, mandalas. Someone should hang this mini masterpiece in the Louvre.

Xavier's eyebrows are up to his hairline. "Uhhh, I take it that means we're good?"

"Xavier, bestest guy friend in the whole world, of course. But I want you to know that I'm so, so sorry. I really am." I return his first sticky note with my response, a single heart. I decorated that one too, naturally.

His grin lights up the room and he taps on my binder with his pencil. "What about the other one?"

I freeze, and Amber fumbles the calculator she was using to finish up her calculus assignment. I knew she was eavesdropping. Honesty has been good to me lately, so I stick with that. "I haven't figured out the sticky notes yet, but they're starting to feel more important than maybe I realized?"

"Finally," Amber mutters, causing my cheeks to flame. What am I missing here? Xavier nods but seems to be biting back a grin. That's all I'm going to get?

"How's Tyler?" He asks Amber, changing the subject.

"Still talking to Ralph on the big white telephone." She sings songs.

Ewww.

Before I can redirect the conversation back to the sticky notes and away from tossed cookies, the bell rings.

I stand up to leave, but I stop by Mr. Winters' desk and put a sticky note on the cover of his book. This one reads, "Thank you. Mr. Winters = G.O.A.T." And I drew a cute little goat on the bottom, too.

I need tonight's slumber party to start *now*.

Chapter 14
Pizza & Promposals

This day... the surprises just keep coming. I didn't realize my brothers would be home before their Spring Break departure on Sunday, and when I spot their rides in the driveway, I race through the backdoor and straight into the largest mountain of boy laundry known to man. The stench of feral male and unwashed athletic gear could make a girl lose her appetite, and for me, that's saying something.

"I didn't know you guys would be here before you left on your mission trips." My brothers are both attending Spring Break mission trips through their campus' Christian Student Union. A generous donor is sending a bunch of college co-eds to Guatemala. The appeal of college grows stronger by the second.

Clark spoils the sibling love fest. "You thought you were the only one who kept secrets?"

Ouch, but deserved, to be fair.

"No ankle monitor? Where're your cuffs?" Then he

pops the top of a Dr. Thunder open and recoils as the fizz goes straight up his nose.

That gets a snort from me.

"Leave my favorite sis alone." God, in his infinite grace and mercy, gave me Matt. They pull me into an infamous Olivia Ovation and doggone, I must be thinking about chopped onions. Stupid waterworks. At the first sniffle, Clark pulls away like my clothes are on fire, throws his palms up, and mumbles something about girls and estrogen. Matt gives an extra squeeze before he goes back to switching clothes from the washer to the dryer.

When Pippa starts losing her mind at the window, barking like the mailman just delivered a dinosaur bone, I figure Amber must be pulling in.

She parks her shiny black sedan in my driveway, right behind my brothers' trucks, and grabs two giant Target bags from the backseat. "You didn't tell me Mary Kate and Ashley were here. Sweet." Amber nods to my brothers' trucks and smirks.

"What is all this stuff?" I grab a third bag then close the door with a bump of my hip. A quick peek inside reveals so much junk food and candy—pure sugar, most of it—that the irony of why I'm stuck at home in the first place is not lost on me. I adore Almond Joys, and I hope my guilty conscience doesn't leave a bitter aftertaste.

Amber pulls me out of my penitent spiral. "I brought sticky notes, face masks, nose strips, fuzzy socks, candy, stuff to make our own pizzas," she bumps her hip against mine, "and lots and lots of chocolate."

"Awwww, Amber. I love you, too."

She grins. "Your conditional love is inspiring. You can demonstrate said love by opening the door."

Right. Those bags do look heavy. "Please let me pay you for half of this. I've been saving my wages for school and..." I bite my lip and let that awkward sentence die off. I use my free hand to turn the knob. Pippa is so excited to see Amber, she practically knocks the door off its hinges.

"Down girl!" Someone has the zoomies.

Pippa knocks Amber over, bags and all, and just as I'm about to offer profuse apologies for the canine confetti now stuck to her shirt, Amber blinks up at the ceiling and whispers, "I have been chosen." Dog love has that effect sometimes. You'd think we've been friends for so long Pippa wouldn't react like that... I guess she's suffered from my being grounded, too. Amber withdrawal is a very real, very tragic condition.

Clark half laughs, half snorts, but Matt has the decency to ask, "Are you hurt?"

She props herself up on one arm and shakes her head no at Matt, then scratches Pippa behind her ear. "Well, that's one way to get paws-itively floored."

The boys groan at her cheesy pun while I roll my eyes and offer a hand to help her up.

Amber is not immune to the scent emanating from the laundry room. She pulls the collar of her pink shirt over the bottom of her face, pinches it to her nose, and waves a hand to fan the air in front of her. "My nose hurts, too. What is that ripe stank?"

"Your upper lip?" Offers Clark.

She snaps a finger. "Nope, I've got it. It's the dust from that antique joke." Amber fires back. Clark fights a smile and turns away. Of course he'd never concede that she's won that round.

With a satisfied smirk, she pulls a giant, equally stinky dog bone from one of the bags. Pippa accepts her offering gratefully and parks herself on the end of the couch. My sweet pup is content to gnaw while we preheat the oven and dig through the cabinets to find a round pan.

The boys leave us alone as Amber sorts out our ingredients and we assemble our pie. The best part about making your own pizzas is A) you can put whatever you want on it and B) it's fun to make goofy shapes out of the ingredients. Food can be art, too. Which is why our pizza has a smile made out of pepperoni, eyes from olives, a mushroom for a nose, and two slices of green pepper for a handlebar mustache. Our next achievement for the evening will be to make it disappear.

While the pizza cooks, we bide our time at the kitchen table as the twins drop in periodically to steal unused toppings. Amber dumps all the supplies from the last bag across the wooden surface. There are an insane number of sticky notes in all shapes, sizes, and colors, foam brushes, Mod Podge, and a twelve by nine-inch canvas. I can only stare and hope she has a plan, because I have no idea what's going on.

"Do you still have all the sticky notes Xavier gave you?"

"Yeah, he told me I should keep them. They're in my binder."

The color drains from her face. "Please don't tell me you left your binder in your locker."

"It's in my backpack by my desk."

"Then what are you waiting for?" Her urgency scares me into action and I speed walk down the hall to grab it. When I return, she's cleared a space. She grabs the pile of sticky notes and spreads them out in front of my seat.

"You're going to have to explain what's happening right now because those are a bunch of notes I drew all over. Xavier knows I like to doodle and these are so heavily decorated they probably don't make any sense to anyone else."

"Seriously?" She deadpans.

"Don't patronize me. Tell me what I'm missing!" I'm yelling, but I'm laughing. My insides are vibrating and I have an urgent need to move. "Show me already."

"Girls? Is something wrong? What's all the fuss about?" Mom comes into the kitchen with a look of concern and mismatched socks in her hands.

"Mrs. James, you're not going to want to miss this." Amber takes my pile of stickies and starts to organize them. "This isn't the Enigma—it's super simple. Ignore the letters for now and put the numbers in chronological order."

Mom, Clark, and Matt watch silently as we arrange the sticky notes in order based on the tiny numbers in the top corners, one through thirty-one. When she's finished, they spell out "I LOVE YOU, LIV. WILL YOU BE MY PROM DATE?"

I'm still having trouble processing exactly what I've read when mom mutters, "'Bout time..." and drudges back to the laundry room shaking her head.

A rush of pure joy radiates from my center and shoots

through my body, to the tips of my fingers and toes. Do I shout or jump for excitement? My heartbeat seems to pick up speed as my smile takes over my face. I squeeze my eyes shut, count to five, then open them again. Yep, this is real. Xavier's words are still there, spelled out in his own handwriting, detailed with my artistic embellishments. I feel so light I could float.

"That'll be twenty bucks, please." Clark groans at Matt's demand and pulls out his wallet.

"Were you guys betting if Xavier would fall for me?" What parallel universe is this?

"Not if. When." Matt winks, then stuffs the bills into his pocket like nothing has happened. "Clark thought you'd confess your feelings first, but I called it. I knew Xavier would man up."

Well, alrighty then.

Lightheaded, I fall back into my seat. Amber is bouncing on her toes and clapping like a toddler. The timer on the oven beeps loudly, but I'm still too stunned to move. Amber digs through kitchen drawers until she finds an oven mitt and removes our pizza, then cuts it and sets it on the stove to cool. Matt steals a slice with an olive eyeball and offers a salute as he backs out of the kitchen.

"Xavier..." Oh my.

"Uh-huh, uh-huh..."

"Xavier loves me. Me!" My heartbeat races and my face splits into a grin so wide my cheeks hurt. If I could see my own face, I bet I could make pizza man and his pepperoni pout jealous. I could go dizzy trying to comprehend it all.

"No kidding! "Amber throws her arms in the air, and

then we shriek like wild banshees until my dad runs into the room, his eyebrow folding inward, nose crinkled. The lines on his forehead relax as he appears to realize nothing is wrong. He looks at the pizza, then the sticky notes, and walks away with a lopsided grin, shaking his head. He mumbles "Finally" as he leaves.

Both of us find this hilarious and we dissolve into a fit of laughter once he's gone.

As we eat half of the pizza man's face, I consider the rest of the supplies on the table. "So, what's the plan here?"

"Well, Xavier doesn't know you've cracked his ridiculously complex code, so..."

My shoulders fall at her sarcasm. "I thought he was just giving me sticky notes to sketch fun designs on during class."

"Fair enough." Her words are kind but her tone is ripe with mock condescension.

"You, of all people, know I would never dare to dream he might feel the same way about me."

"Awwww. Okay, that makes sense." She clears her throat. "I'm sorry for being so judgy."

"Apology accepted. Also, What. Is. The. Plan?"

"Ok, so you're like, super artsy, obviously, so I figured you could use these sticky notes—because, hello, sticky notes—to Mod Podge some sort of response on the canvas. What do you think?"

I blink. "That's... that's... brilliant!"

"So, how can I help?"

"Seriously? You brought everything I need. And you're excellent moral support."

"Always." It's true. She is.

"You deserve full movie picking privileges, too."

"Since the boys aren't here, we should watch—"

"—*Princess Diaries!*" we squeal in unison. My poor parents.

I study the materials while Amber searches for the film and moves our candy and junk food to the living room. Then, *bam*–a stroke of genius. Amber must see the figurative lightbulb above my head, because she offers up a slow, mischievous grin right before tossing a Swedish Fish into her mouth.

"I'm going to sketch out a collage of sorts and if you don't mind helping me tear the sticky notes into certain shapes and small pieces, I'll Mod Podge it, then paint the perfect answer to his promposal."

"Your wish is my command." She curtsies, and in goes a pair of Sour Patch Kids.

Over the next two-and-a-half hours, we sketch, tear, and paint while we quote Joe and the future Queen of Genovia, accompanied by Pippa's soft snores at our feet. I'm forced to stop after I apply the Mod Podge and promise to send Amber a picture after it dries and I finish tomorrow night. Since I'm grounded for at least another week or more, I'll have to figure out how to either give it to Xavier before church Sunday or wait until school on Monday. After excessive prayers, a chamomile tea or ten, and a strong dose of lavender rollerball applied to the wrist to surely calm my anxious nerves, of course.

There's just this one thing I really need to do first...

* * *

Amber left early for her Saturday morning ballet class, and I got permission from the 'rents to make amends with the fine folks at the Sugar Shatterers. Am I looking forward to that? Absolutely not. But as much as I chafe at the idea of confessing—again—that I've been so deceptive, I'm ready to face the consequences. It's time to clear the 'ole conscious once and for all and come clean. My stomach disagrees, as I'm quite literally nauseous about the potential fallout, and my weak knees are making the drive a wee bit difficult.

I pull into the same exact spot in Bluegrass Baptist's parking lot as I did the first time I showed up for Sugar Shatterers. Except this time, the temperature is a little warmer outside, there's no longer a Vanderbilt V hanging from my rearview mirror, and I'm here to own up to my lie, not fabricate a new one.

The revolving door to the hospital rotates me in and I'm greeted by the same information attendant, who offers a warm smile and nods as I pass. When I see Paul, time does that weird thing where it slows down a little, and yet ticks by too fast, too. I have to swallow hard.

"Well look who decided to join us. Our favorite diabetic Donkey." He smirks and leans back in his chair. "Leave your little friend back at the swamp?"

I came to apologize and he's insulting Xavier before I even get a chance to start? I flick a stray strand of glorious red over my shoulder, put one hand on my jutted-out hip, and point right at his chest with the other. "Having supportive friends is a huge blessing, which you'd know if you ever tried to be one." For the shortest millisecond, I swear hurt replaces his usual expression of bored indiffer-ence. Maybe I should have held back a little with the sass.

Paul's eyes grow wide and the few other Sugar Shat-terers who arrived early turn their direction our way. He sits up straighter in his seat and starts to reply, "Whoa, there Donkey, I—

"My name is Olivia, and I never said I was diabetic."

Paul stares at me like I'm gum stuck to the bottom of his shoe, but composes himself quickly. "Wow Donkey, you must have really liked that sign, huh?"

Our audience gapes, jaws open wide, and Nurse Underwood strolls through the door with her rolling cart. "Olivia, what a pleasant surprise. We missed you the last couple of weeks. Your flyers have been a huge hit with our board of directors."

"Um, thank you, Mrs. Underwood, but I'm here to apologize. Sugar Shatterers is a wonderful program and I appreciate you accepting me so warmly. But I attended under false pretenses, and—"

"It was me. With that sign and this face, how could she resist?" Paul runs a hand through his blond curls and Mrs. Underwood and I both choose to ignore him. I want to ask if he was hugged enough as a child, but now isn't the most appropriate time.

"—And I regret that I led you to believe I was diabet-ic." I keep my gaze on the floor, afraid of what I'll see if I look at her.

She pauses so long I think she must be formulating a scathing rebuke. "Well, that's rather unusual, but there's no rule that people who don't have diabetes can't support the Sugar Shatterers." I lift my eyes as she offers a kind smile. "And think of how much you've helped us with your artwork."

Now *my* jaw is on the floor. I don't deserve all this grace. "I'm honored you let me make the flyers at all. Thank you."

"I guess this means you won't be staying today?"

"No ma'am, I don't think that's a good idea. But thank you again... for everything."

She nods and continues setting up. I hesitate a moment, then perch on the edge of the seat beside Paul. He slides back down in his chair and crosses his arms. "Yeah?"

"Ogre, you know what I like best about the *Shrek* films?"

He lifts his brows. "Besides that hunk Lord Farquaad?"

"Donkey is Ogre's *friend*. He shows an interest in Shrek, he asks him questions, and Donkey never once judges Ogre. Instead, Donkey helps Shrek build confidence so he isn't afraid to... to... just be himself. Donkey encouraged Shrek and taught him about real friendship."

A teeny, tiny muscle in the corner of Paul's lips turns up. "Donkey?"

Oh boy. Surely, he's about to say, "You definitely need some Tic-Tacs or something, 'cause your breath stinks!"

"Yes, Ogre?"

"Thank you. I'll try to remember that."

My shoulders fall from my ears, and tension I didn't realize I was holding in evaporates. Would you look at that? Progress.

He dips his chiseled chin, a little blonde stubble glinting in the bright hospital lights. "Anything else?"

"As a matter of fact, yes. If I were Donkey and you Shrek, I would use all my usual wit and charm to tell you... 'Shrek, c'mon now! You can't be believin' all that superstitious mumbo jumbo! I mean, really, breaking a mirror gives you seven years of bad luck? Pfft! And black cats? They're just cats, Paul'"—ahem— "'I mean Shrek. It's not like they're out there casting spells or somethin'. You gonna let some ol' wives' tales scare you? Uh-uh, big fella.'" I give him a lighthearted punch to the arm for effect. "'Life's hard enough without worryin' about stepping on cracks or walkin' under ladders. Let's go have some waffles and stop stressin' about things that ain't even real!'"

Paul's eyes grow wide. "Donkey, did you just ask me out for waffles?"

Seriously? I pinch the bridge of my nose. "No, Paul, I'm not asking you out. I'm trying to show you that you can overcome whatever fear is fueling your superstitions and live with confidence." I tap the band of his *What Would Jesus Do* bracelet, then pull out my phone to read 2 Timothy 1:7 from the Bible app: "'God has given us a spirit of power, love, and sound mind, not one of fear.'"

When I lower my phone, Paul swallows, his Adam's apple bobbing. "Thanks, Donkey." His hoarse voice is barely above a whisper.

Mrs. Underwood's subtle "Ahem" grabs our attention. Her smile indicates maybe she heard quite a bit of our conversation, or maybe it's time to start the meeting. Or both.

I stand and zip my phone up in my crossbody and shove my hands in my coat pockets. Thankfully, my keys are in there this time. "Goodbye, Paul." I offer a bow worthy of mythical proportions, then add, "Until we meet again."

"Farewell, Noble Steed."

Farewell, indeed. I've got a canvas to finish.

Chapter 15
Steadfast Love

A touch of gold paint to finish off the details on the ice cream cone and... viola. This canvas is perfect. Usually when I finish a project so personal, the miniscule, little imperfections drive me to the brink of insanity. I either scrap the project altogether or point out every flaw to whoever ends up seeing the thing.

Not this time. I just want to stare at it. I love it so much.

Let's hope Xavier does too.

I beg Mom for a few minutes with my phone and she reaches for it in her back pocket, then seems to hesitate.

"Olivia..." An odd expression I can't read crosses her face. She blows a pent-up breath out of her full cheeks. "I've grounded your brothers, Clark especially, dozens of times, but I've never had to ground you before this."

I swallow the lump in my throat since *this* is suddenly a giant weight in my stomach. Does guilt get lighter as time passes? Does it wear off or is it just replaced by embarrassment that will forever burn my cheeks upon recall? Will my mom ever be able to look at me without thinking, "Gee, there's my daughter, the one that faked having diabetes so she could pay for an expensive college and told everyone we were financially insecure."

I've got to snap out of this anxiety spiral.

"Olivia?" Mom waves her hand in front of my face. "Are you listening or having an existential crisis?"

"Yes ma'am. All ears, that's me. Sorry." Get it together, Liv.

"Your father and I have decided to downgrade your grounded status. You're now on probation."

"Probation?" I blink.

"Yes."

"What's the difference?"

"You can have your phone privileges back, but you'll still come straight home after school unless you have soccer or work. The extra chores will continue."

This is no different from my actual, non-grounded life, minus the extra chores, but I think we both know that, so I keep my mouth zipped.

"Thanks, Mom." And since we both think hugging is an extreme sport and we'd easily qualify for the Olympics if it were, we squeeze the love into each other. Tens across the board—it's a gold medal hug for sure.

I send a picture of the finished product to Amber and she replies with three giant heart eye emojis. Now to text Xavier, word for word, the same message Amber and I stressed over for an entire half hour when we planned this yesterday:

Three little dots.
Zero dots.
Three little dots.
Zero dots.
This is torture!

AND... exhale. Heart emphasis for that message, too. I can't believe I'm this nervous texting Xavier, my best friend, of all people.

Has mom been watching over my shoulder the whole time? As much as she tries to hide it, I notice the little grin she's sporting before I walk away.

* * *

Amber once told me redheads should wear green, so I shimmy into my favorite emerald sweater—a gem I discovered tagging clothes at Grace & Glimmer last month, thank you employee discount—and some black pants and boots. It takes five-ever to blow out my auburn waves to my liking, but dang if I don't look like a million bucks after all the effort. Also, my arm is now sore and the blow-dryer is giving off a distinct overworked burnt smell.

Worth it.

My usual swipe of mascara and some lip gloss, and I'm good to go.

Pastor Reyes's sermons are always a treat. I love that he uses humor—even if it is in the form of dad jokes, and his messages are always so personal and relevant. I wouldn't expect this morning to be any different.

"Magandang umaga po. Good morning! Today, I'd like to preach about something we all do, we all mess up. Maybe you treated a loved one in an ugly way. Maybe you suffer from envy. Or you've told a lie, and now the guilt is stuck to your heart like Mama Reyes' Ube ice cream. You thought it was no big deal at first—just a little lie, right? But now it feels like you're carrying around a backpack full of bricks labeled 'Guilt,' and wondering if God is over there giving you side-eye like, 'Really?'"

Well, I wasn't, but now I can't not think it.

Pastor Reyes charges on. "Let me tell you, you're not the only one. Lying? Unfortunately, that one's a classic. Even our heroes in the Bible struggled with honesty. Abraham told a lie, twice, pretending his wife was his sister. Kind of gross, but I try not to judge. Peter? He denied knowing Jesus three times. And what did Jesus do? He didn't disown Peter. Peter wasn't canceled. He looked at Peter with love and welcomed him back into grace."

Okay, I'm mesmerized. I can't shake that weird sensation that he wrote this morning's message with me in mind. Except that feels selfish and narcissistic, and this is church.

But his words...

"Grace is certainly not an insurance plan to allow for sin. Absolutely not, so please don't misunderstand. Nor is God's grace a reward for getting it all right—it's a *gift* for when we *don't*." Mr. Reyes picks up his Bible with reverence and opens it. "Romans 5:8 tells us Christ died for us while we were still sinners. Not 'after we got our act together,' and not 'after we confessed everything on the first try'—but while we were still a train-wreck of a hot mess. If you're carrying guilt, let it go. God's love for you hasn't changed one bit."

I've never been a fan of this prickling behind my eyes when I'm particularly moved, but the lightening sensation, the thought that a load has been lifted. Now that's nice.

"Some of you may be thinking, 'But I still feel bad!' That's okay. It's healthy to feel the weight of a mistake. That conviction reminds us to make things right. If you lied to someone, go talk to them. Swallow your pride and apologize. It might feel awkward, but I know from my own humble experiences that honesty will lighten the load. And you know what? They might show you grace, too."

A few people shuffle in their seats and a gentleman in the back coughs.

"Here's one more thing I want you to remember: Jesus is not in the business of second chances, he's in the business of *infinite* chances. God doesn't look at you and see your lie, he looks at you and sees his *beloved*."

A warmth spreads throughout my chest. I think it's forgiveness.

"Maybe one day you will look back and think about how ridiculous a past mistake was. 'Yep, I really thought that lie would work out.'"

He shakes his head, and internally, so do I.

"Then let that go, too, knowing God's love for you hasn't budged. And when you mess up again—and trust me, you will—just come back to Jesus. He's not going anywhere.

"Now go. Apologize if you need to, grab some of Mama Reyes' ice cream next time you stop by the panaderya, and remind yourself: You are loved. You are forgiven. You are still God's masterpiece. And don't forget... He knew you'd mess up, and He called you His anyway. And before we say our final prayer, please remember to save me some of that ice cream, okay?"

While the rest of the congregation giggles at his light-hearted request for frozen dessert, I sniffle back the emotion threatening to leak from my face. Uncle Angelo leads us in the dismissal prayer, and Amber and Xavier both squeeze my hand a little extra when he says Amen.

God really does abound in steadfast love.

* * *

The late afternoon sun filters through my living room window, casting golden streaks over the carpet. Pippa lies on her back, paws up close to Xavier's face. That's one happy dog. Xavier's eyes are glued to the television, but my mind drifts somewhere else entirely, halfway between processing the sermon and contemplating how to tell Xavier how I feel. I sit next to him with one leg tucked under me, trying to figure out exactly how I want to do this.

He grabs the remote and mutes the TV. "I need to tell you something about the sticky notes."

Startled by his abrupt outburst, I'm certain my eyes must be wide as saucers when I look over at him. He's so fidgety.

I swallow down my trepidation. "Me too," I whisper back.

"You... you too?" His brows furrow. It's all kinds of adorable.

I hesitate, then lick my lips nervously. I take a deep breath and stare at my fingers, like the words will come easier if I don't look at him. "Okay, um... I think I—" Uh, groan. This isn't coming out like Amber and I practiced. "No, I *know* I love you. Like, not just as your best friend. More than that." My heart is trying to escape my rib cage.

"You *what?*" he croaks, leaning slightly toward me as if he misheard. His smile, however, helps me soldier on.

I sit up a little straighter and reach for the canvas draped by a blanket and hidden behind my seat. "Took me long enough," I add a nervy eyeroll to emphasize my point, "...but I finally realized the sticky notes were a message. I didn't put that together until Friday after you gave me the question mark." And Amber literally spelled it out for me.

Xavier grins like an idiot when he takes in the artwork. "I can't believe this." He looks over the canvas with such reverence, I have to swallow, my throat suddenly thick. But when he laces his fingers through mine, it's the most natural, wonderful thing in the world. He runs the fingers of his free hand over the painted images of us enjoying ice cream, praying together at church, playing together as children, and of us walking Pippa. The last scene shows me painting a sticky note with the words, "I love you too. Yes!"

My heart stumbles in my chest, and for a moment, all I can hear is the sound of my own pulse. Warmth rises in my cheeks, but I can't look away from him.

"Kind of wish I'd had the nerve to tell you sooner."

I spit out a laugh. "Same."

He places the canvas delicately on the table in front of us and angles his body toward mine, giving me his full attention.

"I'm sorry, Olivia."

"Wh-what?"

He gives a helpless shrug. "I... think I've been in love with you for a long time. And we're always together, I kind of took it, took you—us—for granted. It felt like we were sort of already a couple, but I should have told you how I felt. Then, when I thought you were interested in Paul..." He shudders and lets out a heavy breath, then runs his hand down his face and shrugs again. "Yeah. Jealousy isn't my favorite feeling."

Because I'm a sentimental cream puff, a warm tear starts to make its way down my cheek. Xavier brushes a thumb across my face to wipe it away and palms my jawline. A corner of his lip lifts. His gaze becomes intense as his voice comes out in a hoarse whisper. "Can I...?"

I give the tiniest nod before he can finish. He leans in and I meet him halfway. Our lips brush, tentative and warm, like the beginning of a promise. It's clumsy at first —I'm kissing my best friend! —then it's sweet, certain, and sure. Just like the canvas. Perfect.

When we finally pull apart, he rests his forehead against mine and grins.

I grin back, breathless. "That was…"

His smile grows. "Yeah." Then he kisses me again.

Chapter 16
Mud Boots & Charity Walks

I t's oddly quiet in Mrs. Carlson's office, save for the hum of the fluorescent lights. I shift around in the padded office chair, adjust my sweater for the fifth time or so, and clasp my hands in my lap, anything to steady my nerves. Oh my gosh, I have to stop bothering my top. Nothing says "take me seriously" quite like wrinkling one of your only decent sweaters in front of the person who has the power to decide your future. The walls are still covered with photos of smiling graduates—they really hold a new meaning to me. Across the desk sits Mr. Jamison, a chipper man with an unfortunate penchant for cartoon ties—he's wearing one adorned with minions holding diplomas—who extends a hand and gives a hearty shake.

"So, Olivia." Mr. Jamison shuffles through a few papers. "It's not every day we get a late admissions request from a student turning down Vanderbilt. You've got stellar grades and a killer academic resume. Very impressive." He opens a manila folder and scans another few documents, red ink and sticky notes all over the place. Is that good or bad?

He continues. "I see you have recommendation letters here from Mrs. Carlson, a current teacher, Mr. Winters, and... *Oh.* Oh, wow, Ms. Paige O'Donnell."

Excusemesaywhatnow?

"But—" he starts.

But? Forget this sweater, I'm about to unravel it from one end to the other. I'll just sit here in shock with only my ratty old cami on and a giant pile of one hundred yards of purple yarn...

"It's not every day we see someone wanting to change direction at this point in the year. Can you tell me a little about what led you to consider Berea now?"

Oh. Yes. Deep breath. I spent most of the weekend poring over all things Berea—brochures, their website, student blogs—and the more I got to know, the more my interest grew. How did I miss this gem before? "I know it sounds odd," I begin, offering a smile I hope is surer than I feel. "But I've been planning on attending Vanderbilt since, well, forever. It was always this... this dream, you know?" I look away for a moment, twirling my fingers together while I search for the right words. "But somewhere along the way, and unfortunately *after* I got my acceptance letter, I realized I wasn't really chasing *my* dream. I was trying to re-live someone else's, and that's not God's plan for me at all." I swallow to slow myself down. I'm talking way too fast.

Mr. Jamison nods, encouraging me to continue.

"I thought if I didn't follow the path of a certain famous artist I admired, I wouldn't have the same success she did. Or any success, really." How ridiculous hearing those words out loud sounds now.

"Anyway, Mrs. Carlson suggested I look into Berea and... I don't know. It felt different. Like a place where I could actually belong." I meet Mr. Jamison's eyes, hoping he understands. "I want to study illustrative arts. It's something I'm genuinely passionate about, and your program is... your illustration department has a comic studies minor, a design lab that sounds straight out of a sci-fi movie, and professors who actually draw for graphic novels. Plus, you have a coffee shop on campus. A prereq-uisite for my artistic process."

The counselor's eyes soften as he leans forward. "I can see that this was a big decision for you, Olivia. And I can tell it wasn't easy to change your mind after so many years. It takes a lot of maturity to know when something's no longer right for you."

Yes, maturity and a disastrous bout of liabetes. But I've talked to God about that quite a bit, and I now know I need to show myself some grace, too. I'm still working on it. And to never, ever, *ever* do anything so dishonest again in my life.

My heart lifts a little as I think back on his words. "Thank you," I murmur. "I know I'm really late, and I totally understand if there's no space left, but I had to at least try. I think I'd really thrive at Berea. I want to be somewhere that values creativity, but also, you know, where I won't leave with debt that haunts me like a bad haircut."

Mr. Jamison chuckles, then taps his pen thoughtfully and glances down at his notes. "Well, Olivia, you sound like someone who fits our mission. As a late applicant, there are a few hoops to jump through—maybe just a hop, really. We're a 'learn and work' college, so every student has a job. You might end up as a library assistant, or..." he leans in and grins, "...helping run the campus goat farm."

"I saw the Berea College Farm on your website and think I would look very professional in mud boots." Not to mention there is a seriously cute pair calling my name from the clearance rack at Grace & Glimmer.

At that, his grin morphs into a full-on chuckle. "It may take some time and patience on your end, but I'll do what I can to advocate for your acceptance."

My chest swells with hope, and I can't possibly contain a smile. "I'd really appreciate that." Oh, sweet relief.

"Then we'll do our best," Mr. Jamison replies with a reassuring nod. "I hope we can welcome you to Berea officially very soon."

"Thank you for your time, Mr. Jamison."

"My pleasure." He pumps my hand with so much reassurance I may actually be able to float out of this office.

Is Mr. Jamison a hugger? Never mind.

I grab the thick strap of my backpack and toss it over my shoulder as I make my way out the door. When it clicks into place behind me, I look up to see Mrs. Carlson leaning against the counter of the main office. Our eyes meet, and she gives me two big thumbs up. Forget thumbs up, this woman is due a big ole reverse Olivia Ovation. When I finally release her, she reaches for a box of tissues behind her, lifts up her signature tortoise shell readers, and blots away the moisture from the corner of her eyes. Is Mrs. Carlson an angel? Can angels cry?

Nah, forget it.

* * *

Waiting to hear back from Berea makes probation crawl by. It's nice to have phone privileges back, but now the temptation to check my inbox every five minutes is psychological torture. Okay, not really, but still.

At least I can go to work Monday night and stare at the cute mud boots while I picture myself making friends with the goats at Berea's farm. Would they let me dress them in little kid pajamas like the goats in all the TikTok videos?

More of the same Tuesday, at least until soccer practice.

Coach blows his whistle to start our warm-up jog and I startle when Meagan suddenly appears beside me.

"First of all, what did you say to Paul? Second, spill. I can tell you're hiding something big."

Which only makes my smile grow. "Xavier and I are officially official." I beam.

"About flipping time!" she screams as she wraps me in an aggressive side hug that trips me up a step as we turn the corner of our first lap. Other players look our way, curious at her outburst. They're grinning too. Joy must really be contagious.

"Wait. What did I say to Paul about what?" And now she grins. "Meagan?!"

"He's... he's just been friendlier lately. Like, legit nice

is all." It's getting quite difficult to remember how to run. One foot in front of the other, repeat. If my face looks anything like hers, we're both beaming like idiots.

"Meagan, if I didn't know any better, I'd say you *like* Paul."

Her blush deepens. Or maybe her face is red because we're still running, but I don't think so. "Paul struck up a conversation with me. I could hardly believe it, so I said to him, 'Are you really talking to me? I can hardly believe it.'"

I snort, then stare at her, incredulous. "Wait, you actually said those words?" Then I can't help it, so I laugh.

She cringes. "It's Paul we're talking about. But it wasn't. It was like having my old friend back. The nice one who cares about people. When I asked him what had changed, he told me a talking Donkey straightened him out."

I stop for half a milli-second, then remember myself before a teammate can crash into me. One foot in front of the other, repeat. Again. "No, he did not."

"He did. At first, I was a little confused. I thought his whole talking donkey bit was a biblical reference, but then I remembered all the *Shrek* comments and put two and two together." She nudges my shoulder as we slow to a walk, our run over. "He's working on the superstitious stuff too. Sunday, he came to church with his stepmom."

With that announcement, I choke on the water I've started drinking. Meagan pounds me on the back and continues like I'm not standing there drowning. "Yep.

Just like before his parents got divorced. It's nice to have my buddy back."

"Well, my advice is, if you and Paul like each other as more than friends, I hope you guys are brave enough to tell each other."

She nods. And then Meagan, my non-hugging sweaty soccer partner, gives me another side squeeze. Lots of hugs this week.

After a long and arduous practice, I'm pulling off my shin-guards while Meagan checks her phone.

"Paul invited me to a fundraiser walk for the Sugar Shatterers this weekend. Look how cute this flier is!" She shoves my own artwork in my face, and as surreal as this moment is, it still makes me feel an odd combination of wistful and proud. I really got myself into a pretty big mess, huh?

"He said I should invite you and Xavier."

"I'm planning on it." Actually, Xavier may want to sit this one out, and inviting more people into this just seems complicated. But afterwards, it's prom dress shopping with Amber.

Saturday morning, I'm up bright and early for the ride to Cadiz with my parents. It's strange introducing Mom and Dad to Nurse Underwood, but, as always, she's super nice. She thanks us for supporting the cause and gushes over the fliers and other materials I made for the walk. We ignore the elephant in the room. It died in Mrs. Carlson's office when I confessed my big offense, anyway. Mercy comes in odd forms.

I wave like a goof ball when I see Meagan and Paul.

She waves back, while he offers his signature boy nod. Fitting.

The best part about the walk is talking with my parents for three whole miles. It was like weight lifted off my chest with every single step. I can finally, fully breathe again. I messed up big time, and I hated facing it, but there's this peace now that's hard to explain. It's like all that guilt that was dragging me down... God just took it, as if He might tell me, "You don't have to carry this anymore." I thought I'd feel ashamed forever, but instead, I just feel... free. Like I got a second chance and maybe I'm not the same person I was before, but that's not a bad thing.

I'm Olivia James, smart as a tack and blessed beyond reason.

Epilogue

***F**our Years Later...*

Standing on the steps of Phelps Stokes Chapel, my black cap and gown catches on the warm, spring breeze. The sound of applause and laughter swirl around me as families and friends celebrate the class of graduates. Phones are out for pictures and professors are shaking hands as they mingle amongst my peers. I clutch my diploma from Berea tightly, a tangible symbol of redemption and new beginnings, and resist the urge to hoist it over my head like an Olympic gold medalist. Barely.

Yep, Berea. As hard as I held on to Vanderbilt, I thank the good Lord every day that I can't mess up His plans. And I wouldn't believe it if I didn't confirm with Mrs. Carlson, several dozen times or so, that Paige O'Donnell really did write a completely unsolicited letter of recommendation to the admission's office. It may have been a guilt offering for her horrendous behavior, it may very well have been an effort to keep me away from her alumnus, but I appreciate it either way. My best guess over how that happened? Maybe my little heart to heart with Paul inspired him to pull some strings. But I may never know.

Fun sidenote: Paul promposed to Meagan with a billboard (yes, a billboard–guess having *Doctor Geoffrey Roberts, President of Bluegrass Baptist Health Hospital* for a dad isn't all *that* bad) that read "Meagan, I would be one LUCKY guy if you went to prom with me." Apparently, he did a little introspection and started making a true effort to be a better friend. I pray he's moved past the superstitious stuff.

As I search for my family through the thick crowd, I think back on my acceptance email from Mr. Jamison. "We at Berea College value honesty and integrity. If you're willing to work hard and own your mistakes, we believe you're worth investing in." So that's what I did. I rolled up my sleeves and poured myself into every class, every assignment, and every opportunity to grow. I learned to tell my story—the unvarnished, messy truth of it—and found people respected my courage. Who knew honesty could be so liberating?

"There she is!" Xavier's voice cuts through the throngs of people, warm and steady as always. I turn to see him stride toward me, his dark hair glinting in the bright sunshine and his gorgeous smile as bright as ever. He's carrying a bouquet of wildflowers, my favorite.

"Hey, you made it!" I laugh as he pulls me into a hug.

"Of course, I made it," He hands over the bouquet

and plants a kiss on my forehead. "I wouldn't miss this for anything. I'm so proud of you, Liv."

My eyes sting with tears. Xavier and the Core Four have been my rock through everything. "Thank you," I whisper, my voice trembling. "For everything."

Xavier grins. "You did the work, Liv. I just cheered from the sidelines. And, you know, occasionally brought snacks." He says that as if we didn't visit Craving the Curls every time I visited him, not that I'm complaining...

"AUNT WIVVY!" Oh my gosh, I can't handle the cuteness. My sweet little niece Amelia toddles over for a hug. A brief hug, because she can't resist Xavier, who scoops her up and holds on tight. Me too, kid. Me too. Matt and his very pregnant wife Clara are right behind her, followed by Mom, Dad, and Clark.

"There's our girl! We're so proud of you." The whole group of Jameses wrap me up in a massive Olivia Ovation.

"You guys, you're going to make me cry." Amelia giggles, Clara does start crying (hormones, she explains), and Clark backs up so fast you'd think my diploma was infected with Bubonic Plague. Some things never change.

Mom wipes her eyes and Dad beams with pride. "Are you ready for your big move to Lexington?"

"Yeah, right." I shrug. "I've hardly started packing. Can we get some lunch first?" My question is followed by hearty agreements. A partially starved Amelia can morph from angelic niece to hangry lioness in less than two minutes. And I get to move back home for two weeks before I start my new job at Whimsy & Brush...

I watch as Xavier carries Amelia to Matt's car and Clara slows. She holds back to walk with me. "So, I heard Amber told you to get your nails done nice for graduation."

"Yep. I went for a gel mani. You like?" I fan my fingers out and bat my lashes.

Clara stops, turns, and grabs my shoulders.

Why so dramatic?

"Focus, Olivia. Amber *insisted* you get a manicure..." She enunciates her words slowly, drawn out as if I'm dense. "...When she knew Xavier was coming to visit you for a monumental occasion."

Oh. *OH!*

Clara nods excitedly and her eyes start to water. Something tells me it's more than just hormones. "And your whole family is here."

This is way easier to decipher than the sticky notes senior year. I hug her, or try to—my nephew is in the way —and we squeal like excited little girls who consumed an entire pack of Ale8s. She doesn't jump with me, though. I mean, how uncomfortable would that be?

Is this really about to happen?

It's like I've come full circle. I look back at the car and see Xavier, his smile a quiet promise of everything I've worked for, everything I've earned. At this moment, with my heart full of hope and peace, I realize I didn't just graduate college today. I'm graduating from the fear and shame I allowed to define me four years ago.

I'm ready to step into the future with open hands, trusting God has more for me—more than I could've ever imagined.

And you better believe I'm about to say yes to Xavier, too.

Right after I call Amber Manning and thank her for the heads up.

About the Author

Shanna Heath resides in central Kentucky with her sweet family, two dogs, and a ball python. When she isn't writing young adult Christian fiction, she enjoys teaching middle school social studies or taking Sunday afternoon naps. A sucker for teen rom-coms, her stories have a knack for weaving together the awkward and the flirta-tious, with a healthy dose of real-life complications to boot.

Also by Shanna M. Heath

* * *

If you enjoyed *Liabetes*, awesome! Please consider leaving a review on Amazon, Goodreads, or Bookbub. Reviews help other readers find great books.

Thank you!

Acknowledgments

Major shoutout to my family for letting me brainstorm and dream, for telling me what works and what doesn't, and for your encouragement. Jefe, Doods, Presh Moo, and Builtdiff_4444, you guys are the best.

This book has been bathed in prayer thanks to my sisters-in-Christ at Calvary, especially the wonderful women of *Refresh*. Your encouraging support means the world to me. I continue to covet your prayers as I strive to write stories that glorify God.

I HAVE to thank Ashley Feather, Laura Mason, and my momma, all of whom read rough drafts of this manuscript and gave immensely helpful feedback and found all of my pesky hidden typos (I hope!). And for being awesome in general.

Thank you to Becca Sims for the beautiful cover and for somehow understanding my vision for the artwork. I'll stick to the storytelling and let gifted artists like you make the eye-catching, attention-grabbing illustrations.

I'm super grateful for Leilani Dewindt of xandlcreative for being the best editor in the entire universe.

Thank you also to the YA critique group through the American Christian Fiction Writers, especially Lauren Thell, Angela Shelton, Suzie McKaig, Jennifer Wagner, Elizabeth Daghfal, Sarah Hanks...there are so many that helped make *Liabetes* more than I could have hoped for. Y'all's wisdom is priceless. I'm glad you guys aren't afraid to hurt my feelings—you'd never let me get away with writing poo and I appreciate your honest assessments and thoughtful suggestions. ;)

These acknowledgements wouldn't be complete without thanking God for his abundant grace and mercy. I wrote this book with my children, my younger self, and my students in mind. Really for anyone who's ever been crippled by the guilt of a past mistake or immobilized with the fear of possibly of making one... God loves us, and we could never out sin his amazing grace.

Blessings,

Shanna M. Heath